She took a deep br............................ walked toward him. He smiled then reached up and touched her lower lip with the soft pad of his finger. Swallowing hard, she closed her eyes. "Did you know that the lips and fingertips are the most sensitive parts of the human body?" he asked.

She shook her head.

"Yeah, they are. The lips and fingertips are areas that have the highest amount of touch receptors. So when I touch your lips with my finger like this, our sensitivity levels are spiking."

He leaned down and tipped her chin upward. Scorching, searing, burning heat embraced her as their lips touched. Her stomach fluttered and her heart thundered wildly. He cupped the back of her head and pressed closer, pinning her against the open door frame. The kiss deepened as his tongue slipped between her parted lips. She nearly fainted as their bodies connected and she felt the result of his desire.

She knew exactly what he could do to her willing body between the sheets. She pushed in closer, needing to feel more of him against her body. The kiss was need and passion and want all wrapped up together. She was near mindless and quickly losing control.

Books by Celeste O. Norfleet

Harlequin Kimani Romance

Sultry Storm
When It Feels So Right
Cross My Heart
Flirting with Destiny
Come Away with Me
Just One Touch
Just One Taste
Mine at Last
The Thrill of You

CELESTE O. NORFLEET

a native Philadelphian, has always been artistic, but now her artistic imagination flows through the computer keys instead of a paintbrush. She is a prolific writer for the Kimani Arabesque and Kimani Romance lines. Her romance novels, realistic with a touch of humor, depict strong sexy characters with unpredictable plots and exciting story lines. With an impressive backlist, she continues to win rave reviews and critical acclaim for her spicy sexy romances that scintillate, as well as entertain. Celeste also lends her talent to the Kimani TRU young-adult line. Her young-adult novels are dramatic fiction, reflecting current issues facing all teens. Celeste has been nominated and is the winner of numerous awards. Celeste lives in Virginia with family. You can visit her website or contact her at conorfleet@aol.com or P.O. Box 7346, Woodbridge, VA 22195-7346 www.celesteonorfleet.wordpress.com.

The Thrill of YOU

CELESTE O. NORFLEET

HARLEQUIN® KIMANI™ ROMANCE

To Fate & Fortune

Recycling programs
for this product may
not exist in your area.

ISBN-13: 978-0-373-86318-1

THE THRILL OF YOU

For questions and comments about the quality of this book please contact us at CustomerService@Harlequin.com.

Printed in U.S.A.

Dear Reader,

Thank you so much for taking this wonderful journey with me. It has been a true pleasure to create memorable characters that live on well after the story ends. I truly appreciate all of your support over the years and I will continue to write and bring you exciting, entertaining and sensuous romances.

In Sultry Storm, Cross My Heart, Just One Touch, Just One Taste and *Mine at Last,* you met the Coles and read about love inspired, love overcome and seen love touch the hearts of an entire family. Now, in this compelling novel, I introduce you to Mikhail Coles. His dynamic and charismatic charm is formidable. But when he meets the determined Cyanna Dupres, nothing else matters. Together they find undeniable passion and a forever love that will not be denied. This is the sixth and final story in the Coles family series. Enjoy!

Or do you want more?

Blessings & peace,

Celeste

www.celesteonorfleet.wordpress.com

Prologue

Mikhail Coles had one hard-and-fast rule—he never allowed his personal feelings to interfere with an assignment. And once the assignment was complete, he always walked away. But this time it wasn't just any ordinary assignment. The request came from high up, and he knew going in that it wasn't going to be easy.

She was asking too many questions, and her friends were connected well enough to begin getting attention, something no one wanted. He'd been asked to control the situation. This time he did his job too well. He reached into his jacket pocket and pulled out the note. She had asked him to stay and wait for her. He couldn't.

Instead Mikhail purchased a ticket to see her perform that evening. Granted, he wasn't a big fan of classical music, yet he sat in a center-aisle seat in the orchestra section of the Avery Fisher Hall in the Lincoln Center.

The New York Philharmonic performed, but his eyes were riveted to a single figure standing by the conductor with a small piece of wood at her chin.

He watched and listened, in awe of the magical, mystical music she played. The audience, like him, was mesmerized and captivated by her flawless performance. A slow admiring smile spread across his lips. This was the same woman who had cried in his arms and who he had made love to just hours earlier. Now she was enchanting thousands with her music.

He was a firm believer in cause and effect. Nothing happened by accident. There was a reason and motivation behind everything. To every action there was a reaction. That was the rule of the universe. Given that, how he'd wound up naked in Cyanna's apartment in her bed the day after her brother's memorial service was a complete mystery to him. He had held her in his arms all night and all day. They had talked, they had made love and they had talked some more.

Hours later he'd awoken to an empty bed and a note on the nightstand. He'd opened and read it. She had thanked him for his kindness and the affection he had shown her when she'd needed it most. She'd said she had to go but would be back and for him to please stay and wait for her.

She'd wanted him to stay, but he'd known he couldn't. He was already feeling way more than he should. He'd gotten up and quickly showered, dressed and left. They had spent the night together; that was it. He had comforted her when she'd needed someone—end of story. But in his heart he already knew better. In those brief hours together they had made a connection, and it had nothing to do with their physical attraction.

Now, in the muted darkness surrounded by thousands, he thought about the note he'd left her on the nightstand. He'd told her he couldn't stay but that if there was anything he could ever do for her to please let him know.

Moments later the audience stood and applauded. He stood also. She bowed her head appreciatively, and smiled as warmly as she could. He knew she was still mourning the loss of her brother. The last thing he wanted to do was add to her pain. He stepped into the empty aisle and left her a second time.

Chapter 1

This was her last attempt. Cyanna Dupres pulled into
the lot and parked her car in what had become her usual
space. She turned off the ignition and got out. It was
August. The weather was hot and balmy, the breeze
was nearly nonexistent and the smell and taste of salt
water was everywhere. She squinted and braced her
hand above her eyes as a shield. Even with her dark
sunglasses on, there was still a bright glare from the
intense sunshine. She looked around. Of course nothing had changed since yesterday.

The same boats and yachts sat in their marina slips,
and the same large sign hung overhead: MC Private
Marina & Boat Rentals. An arrow pointed to the left
directing all traffic toward the main office. She turned
to the right. Farther down the dock path, another more
understated sign hung off to the side warning off tour-

ists and unwelcome guests. She ignored it just like she had done the past few days. But there was something different this time—there was no one around to stop her from proceeding farther down to the private dock area. She smiled and kept walking. She was on a mission and hoped this was finally the day.

This wasn't her first time there. She had visited Key West two months ago, last month and now this time. But this was the first time she had actually stayed more than one day. She'd been there for the past five days, and everything about it took her breath away. Over the years she had lived in a number of other places, including New York, Paris and London, but she'd never felt the instant warmth and acceptance she'd felt in Key West. She'd never allowed herself to. She was a gypsy by nature, never settling down in one place for long.

But she knew that life had changed the moment she got word about her brother's helicopter going down. It was time to take a break and settle down. She had worked hard, practiced relentlessly, performed and toured nonstop all her adult life. If the past few days had showed her anything, it was that she needed to stress less and relax more. Coming here was the best idea she'd had in a long time.

Key West had style and panache. The island was alive with the rich flavor of numerous cultures. From the people to the scenery to the homes, the ambience was a kaleidoscope of multicultural delight. Everywhere she looked, she saw the thrill of excitement and life. It was a far cry from her quiet, stagnant world of polished manners and the refined poise of cultured concert halls.

This place was real, and the people were real. This was just what she was looking for, and it was totally unlike what she was used to.

Of course it wasn't perfect. In the past five days she'd found that it was hot, really hot, and like most coastal cities it rained a lot. It was crowded with tourists and cruise ship vacationers, and there was always a festival going on where people partied twenty-four hours a day. But none of that mattered. First things first, she was there for a reason, and she certainly wasn't leaving until she got exactly what she wanted. This was where Mikhail Coles lived, and that meant she needed to be there, too.

She didn't really know a lot about Mikhail. But what she knew she liked. He was attractive—tall, muscular but not overdone, perfectly fit and incredibly toned. His facial features were strong with an angular jaw, high cheekbones, full, kissable lips and mesmerizing light-tinted eyes that seemed to pierce right through your soul. But most important he was a friend of her brother's and he'd been kind and caring at her brother's memorial service months ago. The moment she'd seen him, she'd known he was the one.

He owned this small private marina and the patch of land beside it. Both looked as if they had seen better days. They weren't exactly run-down, but a serious cash infusion wouldn't go amiss. She hoped she was correct in assuming that his finances were lacking. Money was always a good incentive, and hopefully it would work on him. It wasn't that much to ask. Just a small donation on his part and he'd never have to see her again. And he *was* going to agree. Once she'd made up her mind that he was the one, she was adamant.

So, on the fifth day she continued down the empty dock. There were a number of large expensive yachts in the slips, but still no one was around. It was like the boats just appeared overnight and the occupants vanished. Then she saw the gated and closed-off section farther back beyond the dock area with a number of bungalows and small cabins. She assumed the people who owned the yachts stayed there. She also figured that's where Mikhail lived.

For the past week, the gate had been closed. Today she saw that it was wide-open. She walked back cautiously, expecting to be tossed out at any minute. She spotted someone kneeling down beside one of the boats doing something with a rope. From past experience she knew there were at least three men who worked there.

The older man, named Jumper, was crotchety and grouchy with a perpetual scowl on his face. The other man, Cisco, seemed to be in his early thirties. He was tall, dark and definitely handsome. He was also distant and closed off and was just as no-nonsense as Jumper although not quite as ill-tempered. Getting a pleasant word from either of them was like pulling the back teeth from a charging lion. As soon as they saw her they had ushered her out and the older one would grumble about visitors not being allowed past the front gate and nosey women knowing their place.

The third man, the youngest of the three, looked to be in his early twenties. She had no idea what his name was. He was usually quiet and scruffy and dressed like he'd just rolled off the set of the reality show *Survivor*. Always unshaved, he wore a colorful scarf on his head and a sleeveless T-shirt and baggy shorts with sneakers. Luckily it was the youngest of the three men here today.

"Good afternoon," Cyanna said, walking up behind him as he continued fiddling with the rope in the water.

He jumped, turned and looked up at her. He stood, quickly stretching his tall, lanky body to its full height. Then he took an awkward step back, looking around anxiously. "What, wait—you're not supposed to be back here," he said quickly.

"Oh, really?" Cyanna feigned innocence. "My mistake. Hi. I'm looking for—"

He shook his head and frowned. "Yeah, yeah, I know who you're looking for. Man, you're definitely more persistent than the others. I give you that much. But no, sorry, I haven't seen him."

"Of course not," she muttered under her breath. "No one has."

"Excuse me?" he asked.

She smiled brightly again, something she did often when the occasion called for honey rather than vinegar and she wanted to get her way. "Nothing, it's just that I've been here for the past five days and I really need to—"

"Yeah, yeah, I know—I've seen you. But like Jumper said those other times, we ain't seen him. He owns the place and he's not beholding to us about when he comes and goes."

"Yes, of course, and I do apologize for being a pest, but I really need to speak with him. It's important."

"I know, I know. It's always important."

"Look, I promise you I'm not some crazy stalker. I actually know Mikhail. He's a friend."

"Yeah, we get that a lot, too."

"Yes, I'm sure you do."

"I can't tell you anything," he said.

"I understand," she said softly.

"He's my boss."

"Yes, he is."

"It's my job if anybody even saw me talking to you right now."

She nodded sadly. "Then I'd better go. I don't want to get you in any trouble with the others," she said, seeing him beginning to weaken in his resolve. "Thank you. I appreciate your time." She turned to leave, and then, as expected, he called out to her.

"Hey, look, uh, you didn't hear it from me," he began, then looked around at the empty dock. "But I heard Jumper and Fannie talking last night. The boss is planning a long fishing trip in the next few days. That means he's got to come back here to get his boat. Now, I'm not promising anything, and I don't even know if he's really coming, but since you're so persistent I figure you got some important business with him, so you can come again later. He might be here or he might not."

She nodded her head and smiled. "Thank you for your help. What's your name?"

"Luther."

"Thank you, Luther. My name is Cyanna."

"Now, remember, I'm not promising you anything, so don't come back at me if he doesn't show up."

"I won't. I promise."

He glanced over her shoulder and saw Jumper walking down the dock. "Oh no, Jumper's coming. Damn, I'm fired."

"No, you're not. But I suggest you start yelling at me to leave," she whispered emphatically. "Like right now."

He caught on instantly and began yelling at her. She turned in a huff and started walking away quickly. "Okay, okay, I said I'm going. You don't have to yell." She hurried off toward the gate and watched Jumper walk down the dock toward them. "Why do your people have to be so mean? I said I was going. He didn't have to keep yelling like that."

Jumper smiled righteously. He was obviously proud of Luther's stern eviction. "He's absolutely right to yell. You shouldn't be back in this part of the dock anyway."

Jumper huffed proudly as they passed. He was a man of few words. He did, however, grumble a lot. Cyanna smiled as she continued to her rental car. She got in and pulled out of the lot. It was over; today was her last day there. She couldn't afford to waste any more time trying to chase Mikhail down. She needed to go back to New York and figure something else out. It was almost one o'clock in the afternoon. Her flight wasn't until eight. She had time to kill. Having shopped and browsed for the past few days, she wasn't in the mood to do more, so she just headed back to the Key West Gateway Hotel.

When she walked into her suite, she tossed her purse on the bed and stepped out onto the balcony. She had given it five days and now time was up. She walked back inside, pulled out her suitcases and called down to the front desk to make arrangements to check out.

All she had waiting for her in her apartment in New York was silence. She remembered the last time she'd played her violin. Her manager, Donna Van Kelp, had stood by her side in her studio. Donna's words still echoed in her mind.

"Cyanna, it'll come back. Trust me—you'll see. You can't just give up your career and walk away."

"I'm not just walking away, and I'm not giving up my career. I'm taking a break. I've been performing since I was eight years old. I need a break."

"Cyanna, look, I understand your pain. You lost your brother and you're still mourning. You've been going through emotional whiplash. I understand that, but listen to me. You can't just up and quit a tour. Your reputation will be ruined. I'm no lawyer, but I've dated enough of them to know that this may be a breach of contract. You could be blacklisted."

"Somehow I doubt that. And even if I am, I'll be okay."

"Fine, you won't be blacklisted, but you'll miss it."

"I know I will. And it's not forever. But I have to do this first, for me."

Now, months later, sadness still filled her heart. She had played and performed for over twenty years and now she had nothing. Her playing was off, and she couldn't fix it. No matter how hard she practiced, she didn't have it anymore. Few noticed, but she did. This was a waiting game, and she was losing.

There was a knock at her door. It was probably a bell-man with the room charge she'd requested.

Chapter 2

Mikhail Coles steered his boat parallel to the Overseas Highway skirting Florida's southern coastline. Earlier that morning he had stopped in Marathon to see his parents and now, midafternoon, he was on his way home. As soon as he saw Key West in the distance, he smiled. It was good to finally be home again. There was nothing like seeing the white sandy beaches and verdant coastline with its protruding piers and harbors, docked boats and colorful buildings set against the elevated spikes of whitewashed luxury hotels and resorts.

He continued to Key West along the western coast around a couple of massive cruise ships and then steered back, going northeast to the small private marina he had owned for the past five years. MC Marina was his pride and joy.

He was home and already he felt the tenseness of

the past few days wash away. He had been sent by his former employer to gather information from one of his past acquaintances, who would only speak with him. It was a simple enough assignment, but of course it had turned into more drama than expected. Finally, after aggressive negotiations, a deal was made. He'd done his job, and just like that it was over.

He maneuvered his boat through the private marina in a slow, controlled coasting speed, heading to his personal slip. He alternated between Idle and Neutral until he got the boat exactly where he wanted it. Momentum carried him the rest of the way as the cruiser eased into place. The first person he saw was Jumper, walking down the dock toward him. Jumper had been with him since the beginning, and his services were invaluable. He cut the engine, grabbed his bag and went down on the deck. Jumper was there with the rope in his hand.

"You make docking this baby look too easy," Jumper said, pulling the braided nylon rope tight. He secured the boat's stern to the dock's horn. The back of the boat bumped several times against the dock's fenders, then stilled. Mikhail, with a second rope, secured the bow the same way.

"After you do it a couple hundred times, I guess it is."

Jumper looked up at the white cruiser and nodded. "There's nothing like a Bayliner Cruiser on the water." Then he turned to Mikhail. "You're early. We didn't expect you until six o'clock this evening."

"Actually I'm late," he said. "I meant to get here at six this morning, but I decided to stop in Marathon to see the folks."

"How are your folks?" Jumper asked.

Mikhail pulled the rope tightly and then looped it several times around a horn, securing the boat. He stood up and sighed as he looked around. "They're doing well. How's it going around here?" he asked, and the two men shook hands.

"Eh, you know the drill, same old same old, they come, they go and a week later they come back. Number three left yesterday, number six came in late last night and number two called. They're gonna be a day late. Numbers four and five decided to extend their stay for another week."

When it came to the eight private beachfront bungalows, Mikhail's rule was simple and absolute—no names ever. They only went by the cabin number in which they stayed. Over the years they'd had some of the most influential, recognizable and notable people in the world staying there. But the charm was nobody knew it. The guests even came with their own private security and personal staff. Mikhail nodded. "Where's Cisco?"

"He's off the clock. He left out of here five days ago."

Mikhail nodded. He knew exactly what that meant. "Okay, so what's happening today?"

"I'm taking a rental out later, on a half-day sightseeing and fishing trip. We'll be back this evening before sunset. We also have a night cruise scheduled. With a slow hurricane season, it seems like everybody wants to be out on the water. They keep coming and we keep renting, especially the sunset cruises. Luther's taking them out tonight."

"A night cruise—is he ready for that?"

"Oh yeah, he's certified and good to go. The weather's supposed to be clear and the sea calm. He should have no problems."

"Good, I'm glad to hear he's ready."

"Hey, boss," Luther said, hurrying toward Mikhail and Jumper.

The two shook hands. "Luther, how's it going? I hear you have a midnight cruise this evening."

Luther beamed proudly. "Yeah, I did a couple last week and they went great. I'm ready for this. I can do it."

"Good for you," Mikhail said as he began walking down the dock. Jumper followed.

"Oh yeah, right, you had a visitor," Luther said.

Mikhail stopped and turned around. Jumper waved his hand. "Now don't be bothering the man with all that nonsense. Grab the other bags from the boat's cabin and get them over to number one."

Mikhail watched as Luther nodded and scrambled on board to grab his bags. The two men continued walking. "So, how's my baby doing?"

Jumper shook his head. "I had problems with the engine throttle sticking all morning, and it looks like the carburetor's acting up again, I think it's gonna have to be taken out and replaced. No sense trying to breathe life into a fifty-year-old corpse. We're not talking about some outboard twenty-five horsepower model engine here. You got a real engine in there, and it needs to be handled right."

Mikhail grimaced. That's not what he wanted to hear, but he knew Jumper was the best when it came to marine engine mechanics and repair. "All right, order the parts and do what you have to do to restore it."

"Yeah, well, I already did. Plus I got a part on hold. I'm gonna take a look at it this afternoon and see if it's any good."

Mikhail nodded again. "So, what's all this about a visitor?" he asked Jumper.

"A woman stopped by a couple of times looking for you."

"You get a name?"

"Nah, but she'll probably be back tomorrow. Been here every morning for the past five days. She's persistent—I give her that. But not like the others from before. She's got more class, but mind you she's still a pest. Walking around in places she doesn't belong. Luther had to shoo her away from the back dock this morning. Must have left the gate open and she just walked right back.

"It's been a long time since we had to deal with the craziness—reporters everywhere, nosing around where they don't belong just to get a story on you. They don't care a hill's beans about people's lives and what they do to them when it's all over. All they want is a story. If you ask me they should all be..."

Jumper continued to grumble about people having no respect for privacy and how the media fed into the fishbowl mentality that everyone's life was an open book.

Mikhail nodded his head. It had been a long time since his face was on the cover of every newspaper and magazine in the country. He'd saved four lives and in the process had ended his career. Being recognized wasn't exactly conducive to working undercover. So now his job was to go out to negotiate and gather information, hardly the action-packed life he had once led.

"But, like I said, it's been a long time since all that nonsense went down. I say good riddance," Jumper added, finally ending his extended tirade. When they got to the end of the dock, Mikhail headed to the office and Jumper turned toward the parking lot. "I gotta head out and pick up a few things. The mail's on the desk along with a few packages you were expecting."

"Okay, I'm gonna stop at the office, then head over to the crow's nest. I'll see you later," Mikhail said, then walked down the narrow path to the marina's office.

Fannie, his office manager, was behind the counter, speaking with a couple of customers about taking a fishing boat out. She glanced up and did a double take, then smiled, waved and mouthed the words, "Welcome home." Mikhail smiled, nodded and kept walking to his office.

Fannie Hart had spent her entire life sitting behind a desk in Washington, D.C. When she had retired, she'd headed south for a life of leisure. She bought a small house, married the first man who asked her and in less than six months was promptly conned out of everything she had, including her life savings.

She had worked for the marina's previous owner and practically run the whole operation. When Mikhail had bought it, he'd kept her on, giving her a well-deserved raise and making her office manager.

He opened his office door and headed to the desk. He sat down, turned on the computer and then checked the schedule. Just as Jumper had said, they were booked solid. A few minutes into reviewing next week's schedule, there was a knock at the door. "Come in," he said, glancing up briefly.

Luther walked in with a package and more mail for him. "This just came. Also I put your bags in number one. You're all set."

"Thanks, Luther."

Luther nodded and turned to leave. Then he turned back around. "Uh, boss, about that lady that's been stopping by..." he began, then paused.

"Yeah, what about her?" Mikhail asked.

Luther shook his head. "I talked to her. I know I wasn't supposed to, but I did."

Mikhail stopped and looked up. "You talked to her about what?" He reached over to grab the stack of mail on his desk. He began flipping through, separating it and tossing most in the trash. It may not have appeared that he was paying attention, but he definitely was.

"Um, she told me her name. It's Cyanna."

Mikhail stopped flipping for a brief second, then continued again. "Cyanna," he repeated with a smile. "Are you sure?"

"Yes, sir. I remembered because I once knew this girl from Sierra Leone in Africa, and she was cute and at the time I had no idea where Sierra Leone was, and then I looked it up and I found out it was in Africa and then we had this big—"

"Uh, Luther, thanks, man," Mikhail said, stopping him from going on with his story.

"Oh right, yeah, I, um, just thought you might know

her. She said she knew you and that whatever she needed to talk to you about was pretty important."

"Thanks, I appreciate it. Did she say where she was staying?"

"No, sir. Sorry, but she might be back later today."

"Okay," Mikhail said then watched as Luther walked out and closed the office door behind him. He tossed the stack of mail on the desk and leaned back in his chair, smiling. "Cyanna Dupres," he whispered aloud, then smiled again. Her brother had worked with him on a couple of assignments. The last time he'd seen her was the day after her brother's memorial service.

He reached into his top drawer and pulled out the note she'd left him. He had no idea why he'd kept it but he had. He often wondered what might have happened had he gone back to the hotel room and stayed.

He stood up, grabbed his bag and the stack of mail, then headed back out front. Fannie was still talking to the same customers. Mikhail paused and nodded to her. She excused herself and walked over. "Hey, welcome back." She looked his face over more thoroughly. "Some fishing trip—you look exhausted."

"Thanks, I'm rested enough," he said. "Everything okay here?"

"Oh yeah, we're good."

Mikhail nodded. "I need you to find someone. Cyanna Dupres. She's probably staying in one of the high-end hotels on the island."

She nodded her understanding. "Sure, no problem."

"Thanks, call me when you have it. I'll be in the crow's nest," Mikhail said.

She nodded again.

He walked out and headed to bungalow number one. As soon as he stepped inside, he saw that Luther had placed his two larger bags in the small foyer just inside the front door. He stepped around them and continued to the kitchen through the living and dining room. Finding everything in place, he grabbed a bottle of cold water from the refrigerator and headed up to his bedroom on the second floor. He took a quick shower, changed and walked up the winding steps to the crow's nest.

His office took up the entire top floor. Beams of brilliant sunshine illuminated and bathed the open-air room. He walked over to the huge hurricane-glass window behind his desk and looked out the center pane. The nearly 180-degree scenic waterfront view from his high perch was breathtakingly spectacular. Still he closed the blinds, lessening the light in the room.

He grabbed his bag and removed his things, locking them safely away. When finished, he sat down and opened his laptop, preparing to get back to his life. As soon as he did his cell phone beeped. There was a text message from Fannie. She'd found which hotel Cyanna was staying at and had her room number and how long she'd been there. "Thank you, Fannie," he said to the empty room.

Ten minutes later, Mikhail steered his car through downtown Key West. He pulled up in front of the Key West Gateway Hotel and handed his car keys to the valet. He walked in and continued up to the room number Fannie had given him. He knocked and waited a few seconds. The door opened, and he smiled warmly.

He hadn't seen her in months, but she still looked the same, stunning. "Cyanna."

She gasped slightly at seeing him standing there. She had forgotten just how majestic he looked. He was tall, regal, polished and too gorgeous for words. She smiled and sighed. "Mikhail."

"So, I hear you're looking for me," he said nonchalantly.

She nodded eagerly. "Yes, I am."

"What can I do for you?"

"I need your sperm," she said quickly.

He froze.

Chapter 3

Mikhail had always prided himself on having a keen sense of smell, stealthy movements, perfect vision and flawless hearing. Apparently he'd been mistaken all this time. He'd obviously heard wrong. "Uh, um, excuse me, you what, you need my, uh…what?" He bumbled and rambled, obviously taken completely off guard by her out-of-the-blue request.

In Special Forces you quickly learn that getting caught off guard and showing emotion of any kind at the wrong time could be at the very least detrimental to a mission, at the most, detrimental to your continued health. And as such, Mikhail was the ultimate stone-faced poker player. He showed nothing—ever—until now. The expression on his face was pure stupefied shock. Of the dozens of requests Cyanna could have uttered at that moment, needing his sperm was the last on his list. No, strike that, it wasn't even on his list.

"I need your sperm," she repeated, more slowly this time. The door opened across the way, and an older gray-haired couple stepped out into the hall. They smiled politely then turned and walked toward the elevator. Mikhail hadn't even noticed them. He just stood staring at Cyanna like she had lost her mind.

Seeing his reaction, she frowned. Perhaps blurting it out like that wasn't the best idea. Saying it the second time hadn't helped the matter much. "Um, maybe you should come inside."

He nodded and followed her into her suite. She walked over to the desk and picked up an envelope. She turned, seeing that he had come inside but hadn't quite recovered from her pronouncement. Well, at least he hadn't run off. "Okay, yes, I know this is a surprise and a very unusual request, but please hear me out before you say anything. I don't want anything from you, well, other than the obvious, your sperm. But no child support, no birthday cards, nothing that would attach you to my child. This is just a onetime donation, no ties, no obligations and no commitments. You don't have to worry. You'll have nothing whatsoever to do with the child."

He opened his mouth to speak, but she quickly stopped him. The last thing she wanted was for him to turn her down flat before she even got a chance to explain exactly what she needed from him. "Wait, before you say anything, please let me finish. This will be strictly business, totally professional. I even consulted an attorney and he drew up a contract for us to sign. Of course, I didn't give him your name. We can do that later on or you can have your attorney look it over and fill in the appropriate spaces. I understand that your part of the process is quick and painless and I will of course generously compensate you for your time loss at the marina."

She eased closer to him. "I have a list of several facilities around the country that specialize in the in vitro fertilization process and I will fly you to any one of them you feel comfortable with. I'll pay for everything. All you have to do is...well, you know, and walk away. Men do it all the time."

She took a deep breath and looked at him. At least he didn't look as shell-shocked as he had earlier. "Okay, I'm done. Can I get you a drink or something?"

"No, thank you," he said, walking over to the balcony and stepping outside.

She followed. "You don't have to answer me right now. I know this is a big favor, so take your time. But I do need an answer soon because if you do decide to help me I'd need you to get to one of the facilities I picked out sooner rather than later."

He looked out at the scenery, then turned to her and finally spoke. "First of all, men, in general, don't do it all the time." She nodded slowly, relenting to his opinion. "Secondly, what's the rush?"

"I'll be ovulating soon, and I'd like to get this done as quickly as possible. Like I said, sooner rather than later. A woman ovulates just one day, and my cycle is very regular, which means I'll be, you know, ready for you soon."

He smiled, watching her squirm uneasily. "Why me?" he asked.

"You have the particular attributes I want in my child."

"How do you know that?" he asked.

"From conversations with you and my brother. And other ways," she said, suddenly feeling uncomfortable with this line of questioning. She was prepared to talk about the process and the facilities, but not this. This was too personal, too intimate.

"What other ways?" he asked.

She took a deep breath. "I checked you out online."

"Don't believe everything you read online."

"I believed this, it's pretty irrefutable."

"Uh-uh, try again," he said.

She looked at him. She could tell that he knew she wasn't telling him everything. He had the same look in his eyes her brother would have. Her background check revealed that before a few years ago he didn't even exist. There was no computer footprint at all. That's when she used one of those online detective-like agencies, but still nothing came up. "I did for real. There was a lot recently but nothing at all before what happened. So then I hired a private investigator. He asked around about you."

"And what exactly did he find?"

"Like my brother, not a lot. He spoke with a few old friends, a couple of teachers and one of your college roommates, who actually turned out to be your brother's roommate and not yours. But he assured me that everyone he talked with spoke very highly of you. You're obviously a very nice person."

"And that is the particular attribute, I'm nice?" he asked.

"You're intelligent and you're firmly grounded. You have a devoted character when it comes to your friends. You are compassionate and caring with strong convictions and values. You have a positive sense of self and a great sense of humor. You're tall, attractive and, from what I've seen, you're healthy and physically fit."

He nodded and walked back into the suite. "Okay, now tell me the real reason you want me to do this."

She shook her head; he was too much like her brother. "When my brother died you were more concerned about me and how I was doing. The next day after the memorial service you came by my apartment and brought me flowers. And even though we had only met once before, I instantly felt a sense of closeness with you. Then we sat and talked and did other things of course. By the way, I don't jump into bed with just anybody."

He nodded. "I know."

"You were my brother's friend. You made me laugh, something I hadn't done in a while. You were there, and that touched me. You asked if there was anything you could do…"

"This wasn't exactly what I intended," he said.

"Yes, I know. I realize that but—"

"Yeah, but…" he said. "Cyanna, you don't really know me."

"Yes, I do."

"We talked, we laughed and we made love, but you don't know me."

His eyes were intense and piercing. She nodded. "I want this child, Mikhail. I will be a good mother."

He nodded. "I'm sure you will."

"I don't know what else to say to convince you."

"Let me think about this," he said. She nodded. He headed to the door, then turned back to her. "Cyanna, if I decline your proposal, what would you do, find another donor?"

"I don't know, probably. But right now I kind of put all my eggs in this basket, so to speak." They smiled at her slight humor. The tension in the room slowly dissipated.

"I haven't eaten lunch yet. Do you want to get out of here and get something with me?" Mikhail asked. His sexy smile broadened.

She nodded. "Yeah, I do." She grabbed her purse and they left the room. "There's a nice restaurant in the lobby if you want to—"

"Actually, I was thinking about heading into town. There are a few nice, quiet spots. We can talk."

"Any place is good as long as they have dessert."

He nodded. "In that case, I know just the place."

Moments later they got into his car and headed to the center of town, Mikhail found a place to park on Main Street. They got out and walked a half block to his sister's bakery, Nikita's Café. Even though it was late in the afternoon, the place was still crowded. As soon as they walked in, the workers behind the counter waved and called out to him. One tall blonde woman with big puffy hair came around to greet them.

"Hey, stranger, welcome back. We missed you the last few weeks. How are you?" She kissed Mikhail's cheek and hugged him warmly.

"Hi, Darcy. I'm doing well, thanks," he said, looking around quickly.

"I gather the newlyweds aren't back yet."

"Not yet, but I expect them in the next few days. Nikita's loving Alaska," she said, then shook her head. "I still can't believe my girl's married, and to a Buchanan no less. Talk about oil and water mixing. But I have to say, I've never seen her happier." She glanced at the woman standing at his side.

"Darcy, this is a friend of mine, Cyanna Dupres. Cyanna, this is a dear old friend of the family, Darcy Richardson."

"Hey, I'm not that old, mister," she said in an exaggerated Southern accent while swiping at his arm playfully. "Hi, Cyanna. It's a pleasure meeting you." The two women shook hands. "Are you guys here for lunch?" Darcy asked.

Mikhail nodded. "I've never seen this place so crowded."

"Oh yeah, business is great. Sunup to sundown, they keep us jumping. Yesterday we sold everything except the four walls." Darcy handed them menus and pointed to an empty seat in the far corner. "So, Cyanna, are you from around here?"

"No, I'm not. I'm from New York."

Darcy nodded but looked slightly bothered. "New

York, hmm. That's funny—you look so familiar and your name is familiar, too."

"Cyanna is a concert violist. She performs—"

"Oh my God, that's it," Darcy interrupted excitedly. "I saw you perform at the Kennedy Center in Washington, D.C., about six months ago. Girl, you are awesome. You can seriously play that violin."

"Thank you very much. I'm glad you enjoyed it," Cyanna said.

"Oh, I definitely did. From Bach to Stevie Wonder, girl, you rock. I loved it."

Cyanna smiled and chuckled happily. "Thank you, Darcy. That's very kind of you." Mikhail smiled proudly. Cyanna looked at him and noticed something different in his eyes.

"Are you here in Key West to perform?" Darcy asked.

"No, actually I'm taking a short hiatus from performing right now," she said, opening her menu. "So, what's good here?"

"Everything," Darcy said proudly. "Our special today is the afternoon tea. That's a tarragon roasted chicken salad sandwich on nut-raisin bread. It includes a cinnamon scone with clotted cream and jam, sweetened iced tea and petits fours for dessert."

"That sounds delicious," Cyanna said. "I'll take that."

"I'll have my usual, and better send the usual over to the marina along with a lunch special for Fannie," Mikhail added.

"Sure, no problem. I'll get it right out," Darcy said as she walked away from the table.

Cyanna looked at Mikhail. "I didn't know you knew what I did."

He nodded. "I even saw you perform. You were incredible."

"Thank you. When, where?" she asked curiously.

"New York."

Her smile faded. She looked down at the table and then across the room. "I wondered what happened to you. You were gone when I got back. I didn't know you came. You should have told me or come backstage."

"I didn't want to distract you."

She nodded. "Thank you again for that night, for being there with me, for making…"

"For making love?" he asked softly.

She nodded. "Yes, and for making me feel something again. I guess I didn't realize how much I missed just talking and being with someone. I'm usually alone. It's funny. I practice and perform with a huge symphony orchestra accompaniment with dozens of people, but I'm always still alone onstage."

"You're a featured artist. Is that a bad thing?"

"No, no, of course not. I've worked very hard to be the best at what I do, but it's just that at the end of the day, it still makes for a lonely, solitary existence."

He nodded. He knew lonely, and he knew solitude. "That's why, isn't it?"

She looked at him, knowing he was talking about her wanting a baby. She nodded slowly. "Alone in the world without a family or close friends isn't always a good thing."

"You're not alone, Cyanna. I'm here for you, always."

Her heart trembled. The sincerity in his eyes was gripping. "Thank you," she barely whispered.

Moments later their food arrived. They ate, talking mostly about the sights and attractions in Key West. When they had finished eating, Darcy waived the bill. Mikhail left a large tip for their server. They stopped in the kitchen a moment and chatted with Darcy and Leroy, his sister's sous chef, and then headed out.

Just as they got to the car, Mikhail's cell phone beeped. It was a text message from his cousin, Stephen. The first four words made him smile. What followed made him chuckle and nod. I have a son. Feel free to come and meet your new cousin at the hospital. "I have to go to the hospital," Mikhail said.

Cyanna looked at him, concerned.

He smiled. "My cousins just had their first child. I'm gonna head over to see our new family member. I can drop you off at the hotel." He opened the car door for her.

She paused before getting in. "Um, actually, do you mind if I tag along and join you? I love babies."

"Sure, no problem," he said.

When they got to the hospital, Mikhail called his brother from the parking lot. By the time they got to the lobby, Dominik was waiting for them. The two brothers hugged and shook hands.

"Cyanna, this is my brother, Dr. Dominik Coles. Dom, I want you to meet a friend of mine. This is Cyanna—"

"Dupres," Dominik finished his brother's introduction. "Ms. Dupres, it's an honor to meet you. I've had the pleasure of seeing you perform. You are brilliant."

"Thank you, and please call me Cyanna."

Dominik nodded and smiled knowingly at his brother for a brief second. "I certainly will, Cyanna. So, bro, you ready to meet the newest addition to the Coles family?"

"Yes, definitely. How's everybody doing?" Mikhail asked as he took Cyanna's hand and they all walked to the maternity ward.

"Mia's fine, the baby is beautiful and Stephen is a wreck."

The brothers chuckled. Mikhail glanced at Cyanna. "My brother just recently got married."

"Congratulations," Cyanna said happily. "That's wonderful."

"So how's Shauna and married life?"

Dominik beamed from ear to ear then chuckled. "Aw, man, Shauna is amazing and being married is fantastic. I can't remember my life before her and never want to be without her. I never knew I could be this blissfully contented."

"I'm really happy for you, Dom."

Cyanna glanced from man to man as they walked. They were certainly brothers; the resemblance was remarkable. Both men were tall, powerfully built and strikingly handsome. They continued talking and joking. Cyanna began to notice how the women they passed all seemed to turn and stare at them.

When they arrived at the maternity ward, three nurses were standing and talking at the main station.

One stopped and immediately walked over to Dominik and Mikhail, personally escorting them to a private room. As soon as they walked inside, Cyanna saw a man sitting in a side chair with a tiny baby in his arms. He looked up and beamed with sparkling eyes. The woman lying in the bed smiled and greeted them softly. "Come on in and meet our son."

Mikhail introduced Cyanna to Stephen, Mia and Shauna, Dominik's wife. Stephen introduced his son, Esteban Coles Morales, Jr. A collective sigh of overwhelming joy filled the room. Stephen gave the baby to Mia and hugged everyone. A few seconds later, Dominik was paged and left the room with Shauna. Mia offered to let Mikhail hold Esteban, but he declined. She asked if Cyanna wanted to hold the baby, and Cyanna readily agreed. She couldn't resist. Mia placed Esteban in her arms, and Cyanna's heart melted instantly. Mikhail watched Cyanna's expression closely. It was pure elation and love. He could definitely see her desire to have a baby.

If he said no to her request to have a baby, he knew she'd find another donor and there was no way he could handle that. His jaw tightened. He wondered if there was already someone waiting in the wings.

They sat and talked for a while longer, then Mia's two stepsisters, Nya and Janelle, walked in. Cyanna and Mikhail left shortly afterward. They walked through the hospital in silence. Once outside, Cyanna spoke. "Thank you for bringing me. Your new cousin is absolutely adorable, and your cousins are very generous for sharing their special moment with me."

"They're good people," Mikhail said, opening the car door.

She nodded. "And they're very much in love."

"Yes, they are."

"So how did they meet, childhood friends turned lovers?" Cyanna asked as they drove back to her hotel.

Mikhail chuckled. "Hardly." Then he told her about Stephen and Mia's relationship, which had begun two years ago in the middle of Hurricane Ana. Afterward, he continued with his sister Natalia and her actor husband, David Montgomery, and then his sister Tatiana and music mogul Spencer Cage.

They arrived at the hotel just as the rich red-and-purple hues of dusk shadowed the sky. They stopped in the lobby for a nightcap. After sitting at a small table, Cyanna shook her head, still amazed by Mikhail's family.

"Now tell me the truth—you're exaggerating about your family, right?"

"No, I'm not. Actually there's more. My sister Nikita and my brother Dominik." He told her about Nikita and her new husband, Chase Buchanan. He ended with Dominik and Shauna. Cyanna smiled and laughed the whole time. She could barely believe the wild, outrageous stories he told about his family's romances. But at the end of each couple's romance was a blissful happy ending.

By the time he walked her back to her hotel room, they were back to talking about Stephen and Mia. "They seem so perfect for each other. I'm really happy for them and for Esteban. I guess I was right. A baby really does bring the ultimate joy to the heart," she said, walking into her room. She dropped her purse on the sofa. Mikhail was still standing in the open doorway. "What's wrong—are you okay?"

"Come here," he whispered.

She took a deep breath and tentatively walked toward him. He smiled, then reached up and touched her lower lip with the soft pad of his finger. Swallowing hard, she closed her eyes. "Did you know that the lips and fingertips are the most sensitive parts of the human body?" he asked.

She shook her head.

"Yeah, they are. The lips and fingertips are areas that have the highest amount of sensitivity receptors. So when I touch your lips with my finger like this, our sensitivity levels are spiking."

"Okay, I didn't know that," she muttered softly.

"Yes," he said just above a whisper.

She looked at him curiously. She was confused. "Yes, what?"

He smiled. "Yes, I'll do it."

It took a few seconds, but what he had just agreed to do finally sunk in. Cyanna's jaw dropped, her eyes widened and she beamed with joy. A second later she burst with happiness and jumped into his arms. She wrapped her arms around his neck and hugged him tight. He held her so she wouldn't fall. Her joyful glee was monumental. "Thank you. Thank you. Thank you. I'll set everything up and make sure everything goes smoothly for you. I promise."

He released her and set her down, shaking his head. "Wait, wait, hold up, there's more. I want something."

"Yes, yes, yes to whatever you want. The answer is yes. When will you be able to leave, tomorrow?"

"Cyanna, listen to me. Yes, I agree to do this, but on my terms. I have some conditions of my own."

She took a deep breath and nodded, trying to stop from screaming with joy. Her heart was pounding wildly and her insides shook with anticipation. "Okay, okay, what are the terms and conditions?"

"First, I'd like you to answer a couple of questions. Is there another man in your life right now?"

"No," she said quickly.

"Okay," he said, nodding. "Had I declined your request, is there someone else you intended to ask?"

"Yes," she answered honestly.

"Are the two of you close?"

"I perform for his family on occasion."

"That's not what I meant, and you know it," he said softly.

"No, we're not intimate and never have been."

He nodded again. "Thank you."

"That's it? Those were your terms?"

"No, we'll talk about them tomorrow," he said.

"Tomorrow—wait, what? Why not right now?" she asked.

"Tomorrow would be best. And, Cyanna, they're not negotiable."

"Okay, sure, whatever," she said. She was too elated to care about his terms and conditions. He had said yes. That's all that mattered. She was going to have her baby. "Thank you. I promise you I'll make this very easy for you."

"I'll call you in the morning. Have your things packed. You're checking out tomorrow."

She nodded. "Thank you."

He leaned down and tipped her chin upward. Scorching, searing, burning heat embraced her as their lips touched. Her stomach fluttered, and her heart thundered wildly. He cupped the back of her head and pressed closer, pinning her against the open door frame. The kiss deepened as his tongue slipped between her parted lips. She nearly fainted as their bodies connected and she felt the evidence of his desire.

She knew exactly what he could do to her willing body between the sheets. She pushed in closer, needing to feel more of him against her body. The kiss was need and passion and want all wrapped up together. She was near mindless and quickly losing control. Her thoughts were focused on one thing, dragging him inside to her bed. The kiss ended when he stepped back into the hall. "Get some rest, you're gonna need it. Good night."

Cyanna nodded slowly. "Good night," she said, swallowing hard from the sudden dryness in her throat. She closed the door, leaned back and smiled so wide her cheeks hurt. She licked her swollen lips. Mikhail Coles was one amazing man.

Chapter 4

Cyanna let the front desk know that she'd be check-ing out in the morning. She packed her two suitcases and set them by the desk. She got in bed early but then stayed up most of the night. Not on purpose, she just couldn't sleep. She was too thrilled and excited to close her eyes. She made plans, checked items off her to-do list and consulted her electronic ovulation calendar, something she lived by recently. The dates all lined up and everything pointed to the following week as the perfect time to conceive. *Perfect.*

She got out of bed and walked into the bathroom. She stood at the full-length mirror, lifted her T-shirt and turned to the side. She looked down at her flat stom-ach and imagined what she'd look like pregnant. She smiled as the thoughts rolled around in her mind with ease. This was her dream, and Mikhail was going to make it come true.

All of a sudden, her smile faded. She began wondering what Mikhail's terms and conditions might possibly be. She had already decided to offer him money and even if he didn't accept it, she'd make sure that she'd do something to help his business. She touched her lips, remembering the kiss they'd shared earlier. Her stomach quivered as more detailed memories resurfaced from their last time together. She walked back into the bedroom and lay down.

She closed her eyes and recalled months ago when Mikhail had come to her apartment. It had been the night after her brother's memorial service. There was no way she'd ever forget. Flashes of memory and snippets of conversations from that night still stayed with her. Toe-curling, mind-altering, swinging by the chandelier, Kama Sutra sex had a way of searing something like that in your memory forever.

It had rained. She had cried for days, refusing visitors and not answering the phone. She had attended her brother's memorial service the day before but then went back into seclusion. She hadn't wanted to see anybody. He'd knocked twice. She'd ignored him. He'd knocked twice more. She'd opened the door, and he was standing there with flowers, a box of tissues, a bottle of wine and a large brown paper bag. At first she'd thought he had the wrong apartment number, then she recognized him from before. He was her brother's friend.

"Good evening. I brought Chinese food," he'd said, half smiling.

She had no idea why she'd let him in. She just had. They'd talked, she'd cried, they'd ate, she'd cried and they'd talked some more. Then he'd pulled out a small box from his pocket and given it to her. "It's hard now, but this is for the much harder days ahead," he had said. She'd opened the box. Inside was a mini–flash drive on a gold chain.

She'd plugged the drive into her computer. The menu had come up; it listed just about every silly comedy movie from the past three decades. She'd laughed for the first time in days. She'd chosen a movie and they'd sat on the sofa and watched. Midway through, she had reached up and thanked him with a kiss, then another and another and another. Soon the kisses had exploded into ignited passion. After that she'd practically pounced on him as one thing led to another.

She had crawled up onto his lap, instantly feeling the rock hardness between his legs. She'd opened his shirt and began touching him. She'd tweaked his nipples and he'd gasped and groaned aloud. She had started to undo his belt buckle, but then he'd grabbed her wrists and stopped her. The strength and power in his forceful hands had excited her even more.

"Cyanna, stop. Wait, we can't," he'd said. "What you're feeling right now is the impulse to connect with someone who knew your brother, someone to share your feelings with. Trust me, you'll feel differently in the morning."

She'd shaken her head slowly and unbuttoned her shirt. "No, I won't. What I'm feeling right now is desire to be with you, to make love with you. I want you,

Mikhail. Don't you want me?" She had unsnapped her open-front bra. Her breasts had bounced free and her nipples, peeking out from the barely covering lace, were already hard enough to cut diamonds.

Mikhail had licked his lips and hypnotically nodded. "Yes," he'd said huskily. "But tomorrow—"

"Is another day." She'd finished his sentence while leaning in and kissing his neck and chest.

He'd groaned. "I don't want you to think I'd take advantage of your pain and vulnerability, because…"

She had leaned back and smiled brazenly. "Fine, then let me take advantage of yours."

His large hands had covered her breasts, and passion had immediately erupted in a frenzy of kisses, caressing and clothes being pulled and yanked off. His mouth had been on her body everywhere. Hot, scorching, burning, searing her skin as her wetness poured free. She had never wanted anyone like she'd wanted him at that moment.

An instant later they'd been completely naked and she was straddling his muscled thighs. His enormous desire had stood straight up at her. She'd sat up high, arched her back and slammed down, impaling her body onto his. He had tried to slow her descent, but she'd been too insistent. Her scream of pleasure and pain had shot through the room. He'd grabbed her close and held her still. His penetration had been deep and her insides had burned red-hot, but she'd wanted more.

She'd pushed back and began gyrating her hips—moving up and down, pulling him in and then releasing him. Her perky breasts had bounced each time she moved. He'd eyed them, mesmerized, before opening his mouth and taking one into his warmth. He had suckled, and she had sizzled. The mounting force had begun to soar. She'd led; he'd followed. He'd moaned, holding back his pleasure and letting her have her way with his body, and she'd delighted in his obedience.

Her pace had quickened, and their breathing had increased. The first spasm had hit her and nearly knocked her back. She'd steadied her hands on his thigh and shoulder and rocked him harder. She'd come again, this time stronger and harder. She'd screamed his name and pushed for more. He had met her forceful need and pivoted her body, slamming her down on the sofa, putting him on top. She'd looked up, pleased with his dominance and force. She'd locked her legs around his waist. Without releasing her hold on him, he'd surged into her over and over again.

Each thrust, more vigorous than the last, had taken her breath. She'd been weak and her body had shaken as she'd felt the building of yet another climax. He'd pushed in one last time and they'd both exploded, gripping tight and straining to control the uncontrollable. Her body had shaken fiercely, tensed and then sated.

Later he had picked her up and taken her into the bedroom. They had made love the rest of the night and all morning long. It was just that easy, and there was no awkwardness at all. It might have been just as he'd said, a need to connect with someone after a death, but it was obvious that both of them needed it.

Now, in the stilled darkness of early morning, Cyanna looked around the empty bedroom. She had thought about that night often. She knew she'd never have another experience like that again. She rolled over in bed and sighed. Her thoughts faded as sleep took her back to that night again when passion and pleasure ruled.

Hours later, Cyanna woke up with a start. She looked around the hotel room and prayed she hadn't dreamed everything last night. When she saw her packed bags, she relaxed. She looked at the digital clock on the nightstand. It was after nine o'clock. She jumped up and hurried to get ready.

As she showered, dressed and prepared to leave, she began to wonder about Mikhail and the women in his life. What were they like? What was his type?

She released her hair from her big puffy ponytail, then added a touch of lipstick to her mouth. She smiled at her reflection in the mirror. The room phone rang. It was the first time she'd heard it ring in six days. She answered. "Hello."

"Ms. Dupres?"

"Yes."

"Your car is waiting for you out front."

"Excuse me?" she said.

"If you're ready, I can have a bellman pick up your luggage."

"I didn't arrange for a car," she said.

"Yes, ma'am, but Mr. Coles did."

"Mr. Coles. When?"

"Last night. He also paid your hotel bill, so you're all set."

"He what?" she screeched louder than expected. "No, change that. I'll be paying my own hotel bill."

"Ma'am, I'm afraid it's already in the system. There's nothing I can do. It's already been paid. Would you like me to send a bellman?"

Cyanna was seething, but she knew it wasn't the desk clerk's fault. It was Mikhail. Okay, she had to make a few things perfectly clear to him. Just because she was going to use his sperm didn't give him a say in her life, and that included taking care of her hotel bill. "Yes, a bellman would be great, thank you," she said tightly.

She left the hotel a few minutes later. The ride was longer than she'd expected, and in that time her frustration and anger hadn't waned a bit. She was furious with Mikhail for his presumptive attitude. She glanced out the window and noticed that instead of going to the marina area, the driver steered in the opposite direction. A while later they pulled into a large driveway and stopped in front of a huge, two-story mansion. The driver got out and opened the door for her. "Are you sure this is where you're supposed to take me?"

"Yes, Ms. Dupres. I am to instruct you to just go inside."

Confused, she grimaced and shook her head and walked toward the front door. She tried the handle; it gave way with ease. She walked inside. The driver, following, deposited her two bags in the foyer, refused a tip, then tipped his hat and closed the door behind him.

Cyanna stood in the foyer and looked around. "Hello," she called out a few times. She heard music coming from the back of the house. It was her music, her playing. She followed the sound down the hall, past the dining room into the kitchen and then out through the family room's sliding glass doors, leading to the patio. The backyard was glorious. It looked like a mini paradise. She walked toward the swimming pool. She immediately saw a man's figure swimming underwater. He was completely naked.

It was Mikhail; of that there was no doubt. The perfection of manhood had never been so crystal clear than it was seeing him at that moment. He surfaced. In long, smooth strokes he swam to the far edge of the pool and pulled himself out.

"Holy moly," she muttered as her stomach twisted.

If she could only capture on film the faultlessness of his arms, his shoulders, his back, his rear, his legs, his rear—yes, it bore repeating—she could make a fortune. He grabbed a towel lying on the lounge chair and dried his face, then turned to face her. There was no embarrassment, no shame or vanity. He was as he was and it was evident that he was comfortable in his skin. He paused a moment, smiled and then walked toward her. The sexy sureness of his bold movements took her breath away.

"Oh. My. Gooo…"

Mikhail turned, seeing Cyanna standing there. She was pure elegant sex appeal, even in her form-fitted knee length dress. He had to smile. She had no idea the effect her quiet, prim and proper manner had on men, on him. His body began to heat up just seeing her standing there. And right now, all he could think about was peeling that dress from her body and wrapping her legs around his waist. But he had to shelve those thoughts for now. Business first, pleasure second. He tossed the towel behind him and walked over.

Her jaw was slack as she tried to avert her eyes away from him. Her shyness and embarrassment at seeing him naked was sweet.

He knew the effect he had on women. He'd be a fool not to. In grade school little girls had been clamoring and falling all over themselves for his attention. Middle and high school were pretty much the same, but when it came to college things ramped up exponentially. It was insanely ridiculous. They cooked and cleaned for him and did whatever he wanted them to do, all in hopes of calling him theirs. Most men would love being in that position, but he mostly brushed their attention off. But when he wanted to make a statement and be noticed by a particular woman, there was no question about it, he was noticed. Today was one of those days.

When they had kissed, the attraction was still there and strong. The passion he felt when he pressed his body to hers nearly knocked him off his feet. He intended to give her three conditions. He knew she'd balk at the first two, but the last he hoped would satisfy both of them.

"Good morning," he said, smiling graciously. "Welcome."

"Good morning. Thank you." She paused to listen. "Nice music."

He nodded. "Yes, it is. I was never much for classical music, but I must say it's growing on me."

It was one of her feature pieces, of course. She looked

around, admiring the stunning beauty of the place. "So, is this your home?"

"Sometimes, today it is. It's usually rented out, but it's between rentals right now. I hope you're hungry. You'll need your nourishment," he said, nodding to a table set in the gazebo.

"No, thank you. I don't usually eat breakfast," she said.

"Well, that's going to have to stop immediately, isn't it?"

"Mikhail, I asked you to be my sperm donor, not my babysitter. You can't just come into my life and regulate everything. It's my life. I'm perfectly capable of paying my own hotel bill, finding my own transportation and deciding when or if I'm hungry. Yes, I will begin eating a healthy and more balanced diet when I'm pregnant. So in the future please allow me to take care of my personal matters and my business myself. I'm a big girl. I've been on my own for a long time. I can take care of myself and whoever else comes along."

"Of course you can, and I apologize," he said. "You're right—that was presumptuous of me. In my defense, I wanted this morning to go as smoothly as possible for you."

"Thank you," she said more softly. She didn't expect him to be so accommodating to her feelings. "Okay, I thought you'd be dressed to go by now," she said, trying to keep her eyes averted upward.

"To go where?" he asked.

"To the clinic," she said. "I thought maybe if it was okay with you we could get a flight out this evening or even sooner. There's a first-rate clinic in Atlanta that has an extremely good reputation, and their marked success rate of viable pregnancies is impressive. We can go there. I can make all the arrangements."

"No, that won't be necessary. I've already made arrangements and taken care of everything."

"What do you mean you made arrangements?" she asked, feeling her annoyance begin to simmer again. "Did you change your mind?"

"No, of course not," he said. "But as I said, on my terms."

"Okay, what exactly are your terms?" she asked.

He smiled. "I'll make the donation as you requested, but it'll be the old-fashioned way and not in a petri dish."

"What do you mean the old-fashioned way?" she asked, completely dense until he looked at her and tilted his head. Seeing the expression on his face, she immediately understood. Her breath quickly caught in her throat, and her jaw dropped. She looked down the full length of his perfect body and nearly passed out. She knew without a doubt that sex with Mikhail was mind-blowing insanity. She'd barely survived their one weekend together. But there was no way she could, day after day, night after night, oh my... "No, no, out of the question. This has to be done the right way."

"The right way—do you want to explain that? Because right now you're implying that the entire human race has been doing it the wrong way all this time." He smirked humorously.

"You know what I mean. This has to be clinical."

"Why?"

"Because," she said, then took a deep breath and exhaled. "I don't want any residual sentiments or feelings. These things have a tendency to get emotionally messy. I want to avoid that at all costs, thus intimacy without attachment."

"I assure you I can control my feelings. Can you?"

"Of course I can," she blurted out too quickly.

"Good, then there's no reason why this can't work my way."

"I want the best viable specimen. A sterile lab can do that."

"I assure you I can provide that and more."

"I want verifiable assurance of insemination."

He nodded. "I completely agree. For that I suggest we do it as often and as many times to thoroughly get the job done."

She immediately stiffened her upper lip and glared at him. "This isn't about your sexual pleasure, Mikhail. It's about making a baby, my baby. I have no intention of being another notch on your headboard or your latest sexual conquest."

He smiled and nodded. "Obviously your detective has been busy again, and, for the record, I will not be the only one experiencing pleasure."

She chose to ignore his last remark. "I've heard about your trail of broken hearts."

"And yet you still asked me. Interesting."

She looked away. This was getting complicated, and she didn't want complications. She wanted a baby—Mikhail's baby. "Is that your only condition?"

"No."

She tapped her foot impatiently. "What?"

"Our child will have two parents."

"No, no, no, absolutely not," she instantly balked.

"Sorry, that's a deal breaker," he said and headed to the gazebo.

Good gracious, the man had the most perfect rear end she'd ever seen—tight, firm, touchable. She shook her head to refocus. She followed him to the breakfast table set up in the covered gazebo. He removed a few food covers, and her stomach growled. He picked up a tray of luscious fruit and offered it to her. She shook her head on principle. "You realize, of course, you're not the only man on this planet. I don't really need your sperm. I can just go to a bank and purchase what I need. As a matter of fact, I can just hit a local bar and get the same thing for free, no questions asked. I won't even have to say my name."

"Ah, but you've already thought about that, haven't you?" he said softly as he walked around behind her. She looked down but didn't respond. "Cyanna." He gently touched her arm as he placed the tray of fruit on the table in front of her. "I'm not doing this to be difficult. Believe me. I would be honored to have you as the mother of my child. But I can't just walk away from the child. It's not in my nature. I'm not that man."

"Yeah, a lot of men have said that."

"Would Derek have walked away?" he asked.

She turned quickly. "No, never." He was too close.

Mikhail nodded. "I agree, he wouldn't and nor will I. Those are my conditions."

"Actually, I already have another candidate in mind."

It was his time to squirm. A muscle in his jaw tightened, and his eyes narrowed for a brief instant. "Remember, I am your first choice and those are my conditions. You conceive our child the natural way, then stay and deliver here in Key West."

"I can't stay here for nine months. I have a career, a home and responsibilities."

He nodded his understanding. "Okay, you come back to me in seven months. But know that you are more than welcome to stay here with me as long as you like, whenever you like."

"I get full custody," she said. "That's my deal breaker."

"Full visitation rights, my deal breaker," he countered.

She nodded. "Is that it for your terms and conditions?"

"No, I have three," he said.

"Okay, what's the third condition?"

"If you don't accept the first two conditions, there's no need for the third."

Cyanna wanted a baby, and she wanted Mikhail's baby. So she chose to play along. She nodded slowly. "Okay, fine, I accept your terms, and I will be leaving after I conceive."

"Agreed," he said as his jaw tightened again.

"Agreed," she repeated, then looked around awkwardly. "So—" she shrugged uneasily "—when would you like to begin our little endeavor and seal the deal, so to speak?"

He smiled. "Why don't you go get more comfortable?" She nodded. "Oh, and by the way, in case you haven't noticed, clothing is optional around here."

"I noticed. Are you a nudist?" she asked, finding that interesting.

"No, I just don't like putting clothes on to get wet. Why don't you change and join me? Or feel free to go without." He began walking back toward the pool. "My bedroom's at the top of the stairs. Your luggage should already be there. If you'd prefer another bedroom, that can be arranged, but it would most certainly defeat the purpose of your being here."

"Your bedroom will be fine." She turned to walk away, then stopped. "Wait, what about the third condition?"

"Later. Change. Join me."

Mikhail walked back over to the chaise. He picked up a towel and draped it on the headrest. He looked down the front of his body. He was getting hard just standing there talking to her. He shook it off. He needed to have more control, and he needed to slow this down. Thank God the pool wasn't heated. He walked over to the edge and dived in. After three quick laps, he swam to the other side, climbed out and sat down.

Breathless and soaking wet, Mikhail lay back on the chaise with one arm bent and his hand behind his head. The hot Key West sun beat down on him, already half drying his body. He wore dark sunglasses and a smile. He chuckled to himself and shook his head. He had no

idea what he was doing. Making a baby was a very serious matter. But making a baby with Cyanna was going
to be a true pleasure. Fatherhood—he liked the idea.

Chapter 5

"Do you have any idea what you're doing? No, allow me to answer that question for you, no, nada, nil, not a clue," Donna said, asking and answering her own question emphatically.

"I'm making a baby," Cyanna replied anyway.

"You're shacking up with this guy, whom you don't know and whom you only met twice before, I might add, and you're trying to have his love child. This is not you, Cyanna. I know you. You're impatient, impetuous and impulsive, but you're never reckless. This is reckless. This is definitely not you."

"Donna, calm down. You're gonna give yourself a heart attack."

"Of course I am," she screeched. "What else would you expect? I remember the last time this man breezed through your life. Honey, you were out of sorts for weeks."

"Of course I was out of sorts," she shot back quickly. "I had just memorialized my brother. That wasn't about Mikhail. He was just a physical release I needed at the time."

"Are you sure of that?"

"Of course I am. Donna, listen to me—"

"No, you listen to me. I did some research and read a few articles online about grief and the mourning process. This isn't over for you. There are seven phases. And everything I read explicitly warned against making any major life-changing decisions. Did you hear that? No major life-changing decisions."

"Yes, I heard you the first time," Cyanna said.

"You, my dear, are hardheaded and stubborn, so it bore repeating. That means don't decide to have a baby right now."

"Donna, you don't understand. It's not about mourning. It's about me and what I need in my life right now."

"Look, I know you're tired. You've been performing since you were eight years old. You're exhausted. You're depressed. You're mourning the loss of Derek. But please, please, don't do anything rash. Take some time. Relax on a beach, take a cruise to Bali or Mali, join a health club or better yet go meet the Dalai Lama or something."

"Are you done?" Cyanna asked, looking out the side window and seeing Mikhail lying naked on the chaise. Her mouth watered.

"No, I'm not. Who exactly is this man? What does he

do? How well do you know him? And for heaven's sake, I hope you haven't promised him any money. That's the last thing we need."

"His name is Mikhail Coles, and he runs a marina here in Key West. He was Derek's friend, and he hasn't asked for a penny."

"That's because he's waiting until you actually get pregnant. Oh, this has disaster written all over it. Please, please, don't sign anything, particularly anything that looks legal. Oh, where, where did I go wrong with you? I failed. You used to be such a levelheaded woman," Donna commiserated dramatically.

Cyanna chuckled at her friend's performance. "I still am."

"Just for the record, there's nothing I can say or do to talk you out of this misery?" she said.

"No, nothing," Cyanna affirmed.

"Okay, okay, you're officially on leave. I'll make the necessary arrangements."

"Thank you," Cyanna said. "Oh, and I need a favor. I didn't expect to be here long, but it seems I will. So, I'm gonna need a few things sent down from my apartment. I'll text you and let you know what to ship."

"Sure, no problem. Exactly how long is this going to take—a couple of weeks, a month, six months?"

Cyanna looked down at Mikhail again. She bit her lower lip. He was lying on the chaise on the other side of the pool. His body was perfect—strong, powerful, hard and muscular in all the right places. She knew exploring it again would be a definite pleasure. "I'm thinking not long at all."

"All right, keep in touch and let me know where to send your things and the congratulations present."

"I will. Take care. Talk to you soon."

As Mikhail had told her, her luggage was in his bedroom, sitting on two luggage stands. She opened them and rummaged through. She knew she hadn't brought a bathing suit with her. She'd had no intention of this trip being anything other than a quick business deal.

She pulled out a colorful lace bra and panties set. It would have to do. The en suite bathroom was gorgeous, just like the bedroom and the rest of the house. She slipped her clothes off and quickly changed into her makeshift bathing suit. Looking at herself in the full-length mirror, she shook her head. It was obvious that she was wearing a bra and panties. She sighed heavily, then smiled slowly. If he could do it, she could do it. She unsnapped the bra and slipped out of the panties.

She boldly walked back into the bedroom, tossed the underwear on top of her luggage and headed back downstairs. She had no qualms about her body. She'd worked hard daily to keep fit and toned. So if he thought he would shock her by going nude, right back at you, buddy.

She retraced her steps and stood outside in the bright late-morning sun. Mikhail was lying on a chaise across the way, shielded behind his dark sunglasses. She walked over to the pool and dived in.

Mikhail heard a splash. When he removed his sunglasses, he saw Cyanna beneath the water. She was swimming toward him. He tossed his sunglasses somewhere behind him and dived in to meet her.

She popped up a few yards away and began treading. She couldn't help but notice him against the wall in front of her.

He smiled. "I see you took my suggestion."

"Had to, I didn't bring a swimsuit."

"All the better for me. You are stunning."

"How can you tell, I'm underwater."

"Good point." He immediately dived under and swam to her. Without touching he circled her twice, then went back to his original position "Like I said, you're stunning."

She laughed and splashed him playfully. It was instantly obvious that was a big mistake. The mischievous glint in his eye had her backing up slowly. They eyed each other. Each, like a gunfighter at noon, waiting for that one split second when the other would make a move. She turned and swam a few yards away and stopped to look back. He wasn't at the wall or on the sides, and he wasn't swimming around. She turned. He was right behind her.

She looked down through the water and saw his gift, long and thick, standing straight out to her. She stopped treading and sank beneath the water to get a better look. She came up slowly and smiled. "Yes, you are stunning."

"Woman." He shook his head, grinning. "You're gonna be the death of me, and I'm gonna enjoy every second of it."

She moved closer and wrapped her arms around his

neck. "Uh, maybe also I should tell you, um, I haven't been physically intimate with a man in a while. Actually since you and I were…" She stopped when she saw Mikhail smiling as if he'd just won the lotto. "You can stop smiling," she said. "It was my choice. It had nothing to do with you or us or—"

"Cyanna, trust me, nothing much has changed." He instantly circled her waist and drew her closer. They kissed as they sank beneath the surface. The kiss was long and hard, exchanging air for air, and it lasted until the need for more pushed them to the surface in an explosive force.

Both breathless and needful, she swam to the side. He followed. She spread her arms wide and held on to the wall as he went down again and began kissing her all over. He was thorough, but every inch of her body craved more. He came up from the water and kissed her, slowly taking her breath away. He went down beneath the water again, this time he suckled her breasts. She watched until tiny air bubbles obscured her view. She felt him spreading her legs and she saw him there. Her body and legs trembled.

She had no idea how he held his breath so long or if he could breathe underwater; all she knew was that he was taking her body over the edge each time he went down. She grabbed his arm and pulled him up. He kissed her neck tenderly, then her cheek and finally her lips. Their mouths opened and their tongues intertwined, ravishing all they could consume. She wrapped her legs around his waist and arched her hips. He angled himself and then thrust his hips, slowly entering her.

She tensed, closed her eyes, moaned and sighed at the same time. She felt him go deeper and deeper. Her stomach quivered and she held her breath as he just kept delving deeper inside. Then he stopped. She opened her eyes. He was staring right at her. "Are you okay?" he asked.

She smiled and nodded. "Yes."

"Do you want more?"

"You got more?" she challenged.

He smiled, nodded and pushed a few more inches deeper. At long last their bodies were perfectly flush. She could feel every thick, long, luscious inch of him inside of her. She gripped the wall tighter. "You can let go if you'd like. I have you," he said.

"No, we'll sink."

"Trust me, I have you. I always will."

She didn't let go. She held tight to the wall as her hips began to gyrate against him. He began to move in a slow, easy, steady rhythm, in and out, alternating up and down. The water around them rippled and undulated as the motion of their bodies increased. Deeper, harder, stronger, he pushed and she met each thrust with her own force.

She felt the deep swell of passion and rapture coming. There was no holding back; she was about to explode. Coming. Coming. Coming. She exploded. Her body tightened and trembled as she wrapped her arms around his neck and held tight. He pressed her back against the wall and thrust into her again and again. She climaxed a second time. Water splashed recklessly around them. She opened her eyes. He was smiling at her.

"You want more?"

She considered saying no, but she just had to have him. "You got more?" she challenged him again.

He gave her more, so much more. She screamed his name, her toes curled, her body quivering and her legs melting into the water. One last thrust and he exploded inside of her, giving her exactly what she'd been waiting for. He poured into her. She sighed and held on tight. The wall behind her faded, the water around her dried up and the daylight disappeared. All she felt was her body connected to Mikhail and the baby she prayed would come.

They were in the middle of the pool. Her legs and arms were wrapped around him and he was holding her up. His strong, steady movements beneath the surface kept them afloat.

"I guess I have to learn to trust you."

"You will in time."

"Thank you," she whispered, "for doing this."

"No, thank you. Can you swim?"

"Yes."

"Come on. Let's get you something to eat. You're gonna need your strength."

He swam a few strokes over to the wall and got out. He leaned down and extended his hand to her. He pulled her up like she was a doll. His thick, tight muscles were apparently more than just eye candy. He grabbed a towel and handed it to her. She dried her body and then wrapped the towel around her sarong-style, leaving her breasts exposed. He watched.

"I see we're gonna have to go shopping. I'm thinking silk, lots of silk."

She chuckled and shook her head. "You constantly surprise me. You are so not the man I expected."

"What did you expect?"

"I don't know really. The night at my apartment, I guess I thought I had imagined you differently."

"I don't understand," he said.

"Neither do I. So what's for breakfast?"

He looked up at the sun. "It's closer to one o'clock. Lunch is served."

"Wait, you can tell the time by looking up at the sun?"

He smiled. "One of my many talents. I have many, each well worth trying out, I assure you."

She laughed. "Okay, what's for lunch?"

He walked over to the same table set up for breakfast and removed the silver domes like before. This time instead of the bacon, toast and hash browns she'd seen earlier, she saw seared salmon with lemons and wild rice. "Okay, who keeps doing all this?"

"What do you mean?" he asked as he handed her a plate and guided her toward the trays of food.

She began putting food on the plate. "My luggage was in the foyer, then all of a sudden it's in your bedroom on stands. There were eggs, toast and bacon a few hours ago, and now there are salmon filets. I know you aren't doing or cooking any of this. Who else is here?"

"I have a small staff."

"Are you serious?" she said, looking around nervously. "We were just in the pool having sex and there were people walking around watching us?"

"I assure you they weren't watching us."

"How do you know that? Maybe they're used to seeing you walking around naked, but not me. Have you never heard of pictures put up on the internet? That's all I need are nude pictures of me to turn up while I'm performing onstage."

He slipped her plate from her hand and set it down on the table. He pulled her chair out.

"Does that bother you, to be seen naked?"

"By strangers, yes," she said.

"Okay, I'll make sure that no one else in this house sees you naked, except me of course. When we swim in the nude, it'll just be the two of us here. Okay?" She nodded.

"Good." He put his plate down and sat across from her. He smiled.

"What?" she said, eyeing him suspiciously.

"Stubborn, with a temper. Who would have guessed that of the prim-and-proper concert violinist?" he said.

"I'm not prim and proper. I just know the correct way to behave. I'm not stubborn. I want what I want, when I want it—everyone does. And I don't have a bad temper. I have *you*."

He laughed out loud, then grabbed his water before he choked. "You know what? I can't wait to meet our baby."

"We may have already done it," she said, touching her stomach.

He shook his head. "No, that was just the preamble. In your professional terms, the conductor hasn't even warmed up yet."

She flushed as her heart slammed against her chest and her stomach shuddered. She needed water, but her hands were shaking. She dabbed her mouth with her napkin and wondered about the man sitting across from her. There were so many different parts to him and still he was the same as before. She always thought that she had imagined him that way. Nobody could make her feel like he did. There was a quiet, still part of him that was tender and caring and comforted her when she needed it. She'd seen that part in her apartment. Then there was the strong and powerful man. He could look at her and she felt sheltered and protected.

They ate while talking about nothing in particular. Afterwards, Cyanna asked the question that had been on her mind since she arrived. "Why this way?"

His eyes softened. As if reading her mind, he knew instantly what she meant. "You mean instead of a test tube at some sterile lab where machines spin samples of my sperm to get the best quality and then pierce and inject your egg with a needle to perform the act of inception?"

"That's a pretty cold and sterile depiction."

"I couldn't agree more."

She nodded. "Okay. I understand your point. But I think this is even more personal for you."

"I told you about my sister Natalia. She's married to David Montgomery," he began. Cyanna nodded. "Well, there's more to their story and I'm sure she wouldn't mind me telling you. She went to a very reputable clinic and purchased all the sperm from a particular donor just by reading his information, statistics and physical description. She used that sample and had two wonderful boys. Unfortunately, that sample was never supposed to be sold, let alone used.

"When they got married, David officially adopted my sister's sons as his own. But what most people don't know is that they're actually his biological sons. The clinic made a drastic mistake. Yes, it turned out to be a happy ending for my sister and David, but I don't want to take a chance. I want my sample going exactly where I want it to go. No errors, no confusion, no oops, test-tube mix-ups and unintended mistakes. Can you understand that?"

She nodded. "So we just have sex for the foreseeable future."

He smiled lazily. "I can't think of a better way to spend my days." He stood and offered her his hand. She took it and stood in front of him. He kissed her lips tenderly. "All day and all night," he promised.

She nodded. "Okay, I can do that. When do we start?" She instantly felt the bulge between his legs and smiled. "Are you always ready?"

He kissed her nose playfully. "For you, definitely yes."

He took her hand and walked back to the pool. "No, not in the water again. That was way too tricky." She watched as he glanced at the small cabana beneath the far tree. "Excuse me, do you have a problem with the bed in the bedroom?"

"Too conventional. And you, my love, are anything but."

He walked and she followed until she stopped and looked at the house. "Wait. What about your staff?"

"Trust me."

She nodded and continued following him. They stepped up into the tiny wooden room with a large padded chaise that could double as a king-size bed. She looked around at the openness. He released the drapes that were hidden behind the open doorway and pulled them together. Suddenly the open, airy room was private and cozy. He toggled a switch, and the ceiling fan began to turn slowly. It was a scene snatched right out of paradise. He turned to her. "Better."

"Yes, much," she said as she walked over to him. He reached out to her, but she blocked and pushed his hands away. She pulled the towel free from around his hips and smiled at her prize. He was most certainly ready for her. She put her hand on his chest and pushed. He didn't budge. She changed tactics and pointed one finger at his chest and then pushed. "Sit down," she whispered gently. He sat, obeying her without dispute.

She removed her towel and stood in front of him. Her breasts were exactly at his eye level. She saw the need and want in his eyes to touch her, but she wasn't ready to be touched and he knew it. "I like this room," she said. "It makes me feel in control." She tipped his chin up to look into her eyes. "I like being in control."

"Sounds good to me," he agreed.

"Good, as long as we understand each other." She placed her hands on his strong shoulders, feeling the strength of his trapezius muscle. He was still looking up at her as she leaned down to him. "Kiss me." They kissed tenderly. It was nice and tame, but she wanted something else. "Kiss me like you want me." She barely got the words out before his mouth was on hers, devouring as much of her as he could get. The kiss was long and fierce and consuming. She had to push back for air. She looked at him breathlessly and smiled. "Very good. Now touch me."

He looked down at her body and began touching, caressing and stroking her. Her legs wobbled. "Now, touch me like you want me." He grabbed her, and her mind went blank. She closed her eyes as the madness ensued. His mouth, his tongue, his hands were everywhere. He licked and suckled and prodded her. If she didn't know any better, she would have sworn there were two or three of him in the cabana with her. Unable to take much more, she pushed him away. He stopped instantly. His breathing, more like panting, was erratic and forced.

"Lie down," she ordered.

He lay back, and she climbed on top of him. Sitting up, she impaled herself onto his hardness and began to ride him in slow motion. He closed his eyes and arched his hips, deepening her pleasure as their friction grinded even closer. Then she felt it. Her body trembled and shook. She rode him faster and nearly cried from the sheer intensity of her actions. She exploded with a scream of rapturous pleasure. She slowed her pace but kept going.

"Okay, now make love to me like you…"

The last two words never left her lips. She was on her back in an instant. He gripped her butt and raised her hips up off the cushion, and he thrust down into her. Her legs spread wide, then wrapped around his waist and all she could do was hold on to him and climax over and over and over again. In that afternoon, in the span of enigmatic time, he took her body to places she'd never seen or imagined existed. Later, she smiled as she curled her body into his, thinking he must have really wanted her.

She woke up hours later. She sat up and looked around. She was alone or not, considering his invisible staff. There was a note tented on the pillow beside her.

In case you're wondering how you got upstairs, I carried you. I need to go out for a few hours. The tub is filled with bubbles and the refrigerator is filled with food—make yourself at home.
P.S.—Yes, you are now alone in the house.

She squinted her eyes and grimaced. "How does he read my mind like that?" she said aloud, then lay back down. "Good Lord, what was that?" She tried to think back. But no matter how hard she tried to remember the past few hours and particularly the last few minutes in the cabana, she couldn't. They were a complete blur of pleasure. She knew that she'd told him to make love to her like he wanted her. After that everything went fuzzy. She shook her head and got up, padding barefoot into the bathroom.

She looked at her face in the mirror and then at her

stomach. She didn't look any different. But she felt different; she was sore and achy. Sex had never been her sporting occupation like some of the women she knew. She wasn't particularly promiscuous and because she traveled so much having a steady relationship was impossible. Then, seeing the tub reflected in the mirror, she turned.

As promised, the tub was filled with bubbles. She stuck her hand in and tested the water. It was lukewarm. She added hot water, then eased her body in and laid her head back on the padded cushion. She pushed a button and jet streams began to flow from several points in the tub. She closed her eyes and sighed in lavish relaxation. This was day one of their time together. She couldn't wait for tomorrow.

Chapter 6

After a nice, long, relaxing bath, Cyanna dried off and went back into the bedroom. She turned to where her luggage had been placed on the stands, but it wasn't there. She glanced around, then hurried over to the closet and looked inside. She found that her clothes had been either hung up on padded hangers or tucked neatly away in drawers.

She wasn't used to having people do things for her, but she had to admit, it was nice once in a while. For their first evening together, she chose to wear a knee-length fitted slip dress. It wasn't overtly sexy, but it accentuated her body nicely. It was cobalt-blue and sleeveless and dipped slightly lower in front than she was used to. She slipped on stiletto sandals and buckled a thin matching belt around her waist. She pulled her hair back into a ponytail, but then decided to just let it flow freely over her shoulder and down her back.

She went downstairs. The clicking of her heels on the glistening hardwood and polished marble floors echoed all around her. "Hello," she called out. "Anybody here?" There was no answer. She looked around the foyer, then peeked in the living room and office. Both were perfectly neat and very masculine. She went into the dining room and into the kitchen. She opened the refrigerator. There was a fruit plate covered with plastic wrap. She pulled it out along with a bottle of water and began nibbling.

She walked over to the family room and looked up at the expansive bookshelf. It took up nearly the entire wall. She picked out a novel, read the cover description and first page, then turned to the sliding glass door. She opened it and stepped outside. A warm sultry breeze blew into the cool air-conditioned room. She walked over to the covered gazebo and sat down at the table. Moments later she was snacking on fruit, drinking water and knee-deep in a scintillating murder mystery. Her cell rang.

"Woman, do you have any idea who this man is?"

Cyanna knew exactly to whom she was referring. "Yes, Donna, I do," she said, recognizing her manager's voice instantly.

"He's a friggin' national hero. I mean a real hero. He saved the head guy of the United Nations. Oh my God. That's insane. Plus I saw a picture of him and damn, that's all, that's it, just—damn!"

Cyanna chuckled. "Yes, he is a very attractive man

with a bona fide dangerous body and a serious aura of power that's a hundred miles beyond seductive. And he has soulful bedroom eyes that can make a woman's panties melt off her body."

Donna gasped, then sighed. "Okay, one question. Are we talking steroids or is that really all him?"

"It's one hundred percent all him," Cyanna said lustfully.

"Good Lord," Donna whispered. "Sex repeatedly with that body."

"We're actually doing it for a reason, Donna."

"Yeah, yeah, I know. To have a baby. But seriously, girl—sex repeatedly with that body, damn. So, does he have any brothers?"

"Yes, a doctor, but he just recently got married."

"Cousins?" Donna asked.

"I just met one of his cousins. His name is Stephen. He and his wife just had an adorable baby boy."

"Okay, friends, business associates, gym buddies or college roommates—hell, you know I'm not that picky," Donna added.

Cyanna laughed out loud.

"Wait. Is he there with you now?"

"No, he's at work. He'll be back later this evening."

Donna sighed. "Okay, okay, actually I do have a legitimate business reason for calling you. Your Arabian Prince Charming wants to set up a performance as soon as possible."

"He's not Arabian—he's from Qatar. He's not my Prince Charming, and I'm on break. I can't."

"Cyanna, are you serious?"

"Yes, absolutely, this is too important."

"Okay, I understand that, but what happens later, in a year when you want to go back to work? You can't turn private clients and patrons on and off like a light switch. Ammar may not ask you back."

"That's a chance I'll have to take."

"Are you sure? I'd hate to lose him as a patron."

"I can't worry about that right now."

"Understood. I'll give him your answer. But between you and me, I have a feeling he's not in the habit of hearing 'no thanks' very often. The man has a thing for you, and you know it."

"I'm not his type. I know that, too. Gorgeous or not, filthy rich or not, royalty or not, there's no way I could live my life as a subservient wife or mistress or concubine or whatever they're called these days. Talk to you later." She ended the call and went back to the murder mystery.

"Do you have any idea how enticing you look sitting there?"

Cyanna gasped, then looked up at Mikhail standing in the doorway.

"Hi," she said, putting the book down on the table.

"Hi," he said, walking over to her. "I didn't mean to startle or disturb you."

"No, you didn't. You're not. I was just reading this book."

He tilted his head with interest. She turned the book and showed him the cover. He nodded. "It's a good story, very engrossing. Do you want to know the ending?"

She grimaced. "No, of course not. What's the fun in that?"

"Sometimes the endings are the best part," he said. "They aren't always what we expect."

"And sometimes they are," she said.

"Trust me, not this story. It has a very unexpected ending."

"Still, reading and getting there is the best part."

He nodded. "As you like. So, how was your nap?"

"It was good. I guess I didn't realize I was so tired."

"And your bath?" he asked.

"Perfect, thank you," she said. "How did you know I like taking bubble baths after a nap" she asked, then stopped, remembering. They had made love, napped and taken a bath together at her apartment months ago. "Oh, never mind."

Mikhail smiled. "Are you hungry?" he asked.

"Yeah, a little bit. Would you like to go out for dinner?"

"Actually I was thinking we could stay in tonight."

"Okay, we can do that. But I should warn you, I haven't cooked in a while. I usually order in when I'm at home."

"Yeah, me, too, but I do grill. I picked up a couple of steaks."

She grimaced. "I don't eat red meat," she said. "Sorry."

"Good to know since I picked up a couple of salmon steaks. I hope fish is okay."

"Yes, fish is fine. I love salmon."

"Good, why don't you come help me in the kitchen?" He offered his hand to help her stand.

She stood. He held tight to her hand and pulled her back into his arms. He wrapped his arm around her waist, held her close and whispered, "You look beautiful this evening."

"Thank you. And you have on clothes."

He chuckled. "Yeah, I do, for now."

The deep rich sound of his voice made her body start tingling inside. He pulled her closer into his arms. Her nipples hardened as he pressed his hips against hers. He kissed her neck and tenderly trailed more kisses around her ear to her cheek and then to her mouth.

"This dress is killing me. It's making me want to make love to you right here, right now," he whispered as he stroked the full length of her back.

Her heart began to beat quickly. "How? I'm completely covered up. Most men are sexually visual. They're aroused by what they see. This dress is down to my knees with a high neckline and it's—"

"Do you really think that matters? Trust me, the higher the neckline, the longer the hem, the more tantalizing you are," he said, smiling and gazing admiringly into her eyes. "And in case you hadn't noticed, I'm not most men."

"Yeah, I noticed."

"Good."

"So I guess I could wear a micro mini and a tube top then."

"Actually, I think that'll work just fine, too."

Her stomach twisted and shuddered as she licked her

lips. She felt his body come to life and gasped quietly. "I have a feeling we're gonna skip dinner and go right to breakfast again. Which actually isn't such a bad idea, since the more we're together physically, the better the odds are I'll get pregnant sooner. And according to my electronic ovulation calendar, next week is optimal for me to conceive. That means the next few days are vital. So why don't we skip dinner and go upstairs?"

He bit his lower lip and shook his head. "Tempting, very tempting, but you need to keep up your strength."

"I'm fine."

"We have all the time in the world," he said. He zipped her dress back up. She glanced over her shoulder. She had no idea when and hadn't even felt it when he had zipped her dress down.

"When did you…?"

He smiled. "Let's go." They went back into the kitchen. He divided the chores. Cyanna made the salad, while Mikhail prepared the food on the inside cooktop grill. Afterward she kept him company sitting at the counter. She was surprised that he actually knew his way around the kitchen. A half hour later Cyanna set the table outside and Mikhail brought their dinner out and lit the candles set in tall glass hurricane shades around the patio. They sat, ate and talked about their travels and their favorite places. After dinner they cleaned up the kitchen, then went back outside.

Dusk had long settled, and the sun had set beyond the trees. They sat on the double chaise, looking out at the spectacular view. Muted light from the candles and soft landscape lighting around the pool and hanging from the trees illuminated the area just enough to set the mood. It was the perfect evening.

"Are you ever going to tell me the third condition?"

"Yes."

"When?" she asked.

"When you're ready to hear it," he said.

"I'm ready now," she insisted. He didn't respond. She knew he wouldn't. "Okay, so exactly how involved in my child's life do you intend to be? Once a month visitation or just a Father's Day card in June?"

"In *our* child's life," he corrected. "I intend to be very involved, daily, hourly involved."

"That might be a problem. What if I'm seeing someone?"

He turned quickly. His eyes narrowed; then he saw her humorous expression. "Not funny." She chuckled. "So I know you're a world-renowned artist and you started playing the violin when you were very young. Tell me about being a professional violinist."

"What do you want to know?" she asked.

"How do you get your concert jobs? Do conductors call you?"

"No. I have an artist manager. She arranges my larger-venue tour dates with orchestras and ensembles a year in advance. I'm contracted and they pay me a floating artist fee. My smaller hall performances are usually set according to my availability. I also receive solo and private engagement invitations to perform. If it fits into my schedule, I agree to go."

"So you're paid per performance."

"More like per engagement, which is usually two to

three performances at a time. But it can also depend on the type of engagement and performance requested. Financially I can make more money doing a onetime private engagement than a three-night concerto in a major venue performance."

"How often do you perform?"

"That depends, usually once or twice a month during my touring season, sometimes more and sometimes less."

"And what do you do when you're not performing?" he asked.

"I mentor. I teach. I practice. I try to get better. I learn new music."

"And you play a Stradivarius, correct?"

"Yes, I do."

"They're pretty pricey."

"Classic performers at a certain career level don't actually own their instruments. They're loaned to them from syndicates, companies and very rich patrons."

"I read about a violin called a Guarneri del Gesù."

"I'm impressed. Most people think all violins look and sound alike. But it's the sound quality and instrument tone that separates them. A Guarneri del Gesù is an exquisite instrument. It's as perfect as a violin can be. And it's very rare. There are only about one hundred and forty in existence. In comparison, there are about six hundred Stradivarii. Both instruments cost well over a million dollars and very rarely come available."

"Why is that?"

"They're usually bought by very wealthy patrons,

lent out to musicians and passed down through the generations."

"Who owns your instrument?" he asked.

She smiled. "A friend," she said cryptically.

Mikhail nodded. She didn't have to elaborate. He knew exactly who the friend was, Ammar Robah and his grandfather, Aziz. "What would you be doing if you hadn't picked up a violin?"

She opened her mouth, then closed it. His previous questions were all pretty common. Her answers were all interview safe. She'd been asked those same questions a hundred times, so they were no big deal. She didn't even have to think to answer. But this question was completely out of the blue. She shook her head. "Wow, that's an interesting question. No one's ever asked me that before. To tell you the truth, I don't know. I have no idea what I'd be doing. What about you?"

"What do you mean?"

"Was it hard to suddenly change careers overnight?"

Mikhail looked at her, wondering exactly how much she knew about him and what he did for a living. "Yes. It was hard. I thought I'd be in service until I retired."

"But it didn't happen that way."

"No, it didn't."

"Still, in the process your bravery made you a national hero."

He shook his head. "Not what I intended."

"When you single-handedly rescue the secretary-general of the United Nations and his family and it's caught on video by a vacationing photojournalist and then goes viral on the internet, you tend to get noticed, a lot."

"Again, not what I intended. I was just doing my job. I had no idea the civilian was videotaping me."

"It sounds like you regret what happened."

"Just the notoriety that came afterward," he said. "That one ten-minute video changed everything for me. My life was no longer my own anymore. My job and the people I worked with were in jeopardy. I had no choice but to walk away. I was hounded for interviews for months. I still get news people coming here looking for a story."

"I don't remember you ever doing an interview. Did you?"

"No, not even with my sister Tatiana," he said. "She never asked, and I know her editors and publisher hounded her about getting one. But she knows me too well. When I signed my name on the line I belonged to this country. You never betray that, certainly not for fifteen minutes of fame and a couple of bucks."

"Integrity, not at all surprising. You're a remarkable man, Mikhail Coles," she said. He smiled tightly, obviously embarrassed by the compliment. "Are you blushing?"

"Hardly," he said, deepening his voice. "Men don't blush."

"Sure they don't. So, do you miss the job?"

"Yes, sometimes," he said truthfully.

"Would you ever go back?"

"Interesting question," he said evasively, looking away. She noticed he didn't actually answer her, but she decided not to push it. "I know you were colleagues and friends, but how well did you know my brother?" she asked instead.

He turned and looked back at her. "Well enough."

"How well is that?" she asked, guessing he wouldn't answer.

"We worked together a few times."

"Did he ever talk about me?"

"Let me think. Yeah, he did, but only nonstop," he assured her.

She smiled happily. "Did you know about his past?" she asked.

"What about it?"

"He could sometimes be a little impulsive and fearless, some said reckless with the tendency to take the term *bad boy* a bit too far."

"What do you mean?"

"He had a hair-trigger temper, and that got him in trouble."

"What kind of trouble?"

"Well, after our parents died in a car accident, our dad's brother, Jimmy, took us in. I was eight and Derek was sixteen. He and Derek did not get along from the beginning. Derek was strong, tall and angry most of the time. Our uncle Jimmy had no idea what to do with two kids living with him. So he just went about his usual life, having parties and doing whatever."

"What exactly is whatever?" Mikhail asked.

"Drinking, gambling, women. And he had parties, a lot of them. And also his friends would stop by and hang out playing cards all night. Two weeks before we were sent to foster care, Jimmy had a poker game and there was a huge fight. Derek beat this guy really badly."

"What started the fight?"

"One of Jimmy's friends got…" She paused, choking up, and took a deep breath. "He got overly friendly with me. I hit him and kicked him. He punched me and knocked me down. When he tried to get on top of me, I screamed. Derek ran in and he went crazy on that guy. It took four grown men to pull Derek off him. Derek beat him bad with his fists. There was blood everywhere. The guy was so bad off they had to call an ambulance. The police came and took Derek. The guy didn't want to press charges.

"Nobody listened to me at first when I said Derek was defending me from the guy. See, our uncle's friend was an assistant D.A. and Sunday school teacher and he lied through his teeth. The police put Derek in juvenile hall. Then a social worker saw my scratches on the guy's face and his blood under my nails. She filed a report to a sympathetic judge and things blew up. Apparently Jimmy's friend had a history of sexual assault, but they kept covering it up to protect him and the job.

"They tried to bury it again, but the social worker threatened to go to the press. They didn't charge Derek with anything, half because he was a minor and half because it would have been a PR nightmare. We were removed from Jimmy's house and taken to foster care the next week."

"And this upstanding citizen, what happened to him?"

"He was shot breaking into a woman's house. She

wasn't home, but her young teenage daughter was. He insisted he lost his keys and thought it was his house—he was breaking into. Of course his house was eight blocks away and looked nothing like the woman's house. I heard he's paralyzed from the waist down, in a wheelchair and still denies everything even though they found pornography on his work computer and his cell phone showed he'd been stalking the woman and her daughter for weeks."

"The social worker, she's the one who introduced you to the violin, right?" he said.

"How did you know that a social worker introduced me to the violin?" she asked.

"You're not the only one who checks up on people. I looked you up online. Your Wikipedia page was very informative."

She nodded. "Yes, she was. She used to listen to classical music in her office. It was the first time I'd ever heard music like that. I was amazed. She saw that I loved it. One of her nephews had to play the violin in school and he hated it. She asked me if I'd like to try it. I'd listened to her music so much that as soon as I touched it, I knew exactly what to do and how each string sounded." She smiled, remembering.

"Mrs. Hunter called me a savant. At the time I had no idea what that even was. But she said I inhaled the music like breathing and that playing the violin was the only thing that calmed my heart. Her husband was a Baptist preacher, and they had a house full of foster kids. They took us in. Derek stayed for a few years, then enlisted. He knew I'd be safe with them. They got me lessons, and after a while I started teaching the teacher. Then I went to Juilliard Pre-College Division."

"So you studied at Juilliard."

"For a while, yes, then I transferred to the Curtis Institute of Music in Philadelphia. It's more exclusive and it's the best and hardest college in which to be admitted.

"I received a recording contract when I was fifteen. My solo debut performance with the Philadelphia Philharmonic followed."

"Impressive. And what about Uncle Jimmy?" he asked.

She shrugged. "Imagine his surprise when he found out that his niece was a classical musician. We didn't speak for a long time after that. Then, surprisingly, about four years ago he called my manager and asked me to have dinner with him. I went. He apologized for not believing me. I hear he still has his parties and whatever."

"Did he want money from you when he called?" Mikhail asked.

She shook her head. "No, he never asked for a penny. I heard from him again right after Derek's memorial service. He didn't want to come because he thought Derek still blamed him for what happened that night." She stopped and looked away, then back at him. "Crazy family drama, huh?" she said softly.

"No, not at all," he said, standing with his hand out to her.

She stood with him, and he held her tight. She exhaled and melted into his embrace. "I blamed myself for a long time."

"What?"

"For what happened to Derek," she said. "I blamed myself."

"You were a kid. Derek was a kid. You were both blameless."

"No, I mean afterward, with Derek's death. I should have stopped him. He told me he was going to be away for a while and he didn't know how the job would end. He looked worried. I should have stopped him. I should have talked him out of going."

Mikhail held her away and looked into her tearful eyes. "You couldn't have and you can't blame yourself for Derek's life and his choices. He chose to join and serve his country. He knew the risks—we all do."

Cyanna shook her head. "Had I said something more maybe—"

"No," Mikhail said. "Listen to me. Derek would never want you to blame yourself for his choice. You have to let this go."

She shook her head. "I need to know what happened. His helicopter went down in South America and he was presumed dead. What is that? Presumed dead means nothing. He was there and then he was just gone. People don't just disappear off the face of the earth. For all I know, he's still alive somewhere and trying to get home. I need to know what really happened to him."

"Cyanna, you have to let it go."

"How can you say that? How can I possibly just let it go?"

Mikhail took a deep breath. He wanted to say so

much, but he knew he couldn't. "You will because you have to."

"No," she said, pushing back away from him and out of his embrace. "I don't. I refuse." She turned her back and walked away to stand at the edge of the pool. He came and stood behind her.

"Cyanna, I didn't mean to imply—"

"No, you didn't. I'm sorry, it was me. I overreacted. It's just—" she paused and took a deep breath "—it still hurts so much."

"I know," he said softly. They fell into silence as the remnants of the conversation hung between them. Cyanna looked out into the darkness, realizing this was the first time she'd told anyone about what had happened to them that night when she was eight. Not even her best friend and manager knew. But for some reason telling Mikhail felt right.

"He saved my life," Mikhail said.

She turned around. "Derek? When? How?"

"It was a while ago. I owe him."

She smirked. "And I'm the paid-in-full debt, aren't I?"

"No. You're the woman who's going to carry my child," he said tenderly. "Come on, it's been a long day. Let's go to bed."

They walked back into the house. He held her hand and she followed him up to the bedroom they now shared. Even though they'd said they would, they didn't make love that evening. They just met in the middle of his king-size bed and held each other.

A few hours later Mikhail opened his eyes and

looked around. Cyanna had rolled over to the far side of the bed. He leaned up and watched her sleep for a few minutes. The calm, steady sound of her breathing relaxed him. He lay back down, closed his eyes and smiled to himself. This was exactly what he wanted, a normal life—waking up with a woman he cared about in his bed. At thirty-five years old he had done his duty, had his fun and made his fortune. Now it was time for him to take a break from all that. He needed stability and a sense of permanence. His cousin, his sisters and even his brother had settled down. It was his time.

He had bought land and built this home a long time ago but had seldom stayed there, choosing instead to rent it out and live at the marina. For him this wasn't just a house. It was a home. It was a place for a family to live and grow. Now it would become the place for his family. He glanced over at Cyanna again. The problem was having her in his arms and in his bed felt too right, too soon. He knew nothing could be that right. It was the same feeling he'd had when he'd first met her in New York. Being with her drew him in too quickly.

They called it an instant attraction or love at first sight. He didn't buy it. No woman had ever turned his head like this before. Why her? Why now? But he couldn't deny that she made him feel complete. Seeing Cyanna, being with her made him helplessly open his heart. She overwhelmed him, and he was willfully letting her. He didn't just want to care for and protect her, he wanted to love her. The thought staggered him instantly. He got up and went downstairs.

Cyanna woke up. She reached out and felt around

for Mikhail, but he wasn't there. She sat up and looked around the room. There was just enough light to see that she was alone. She waited a few minutes, then got out of bed and peeked into the bathroom. He wasn't there. Assuming he was outside at the pool, she slipped out of her oversize sleep T-shirt and put on the silk robe hanging on the back of the door. She walked out into the hall and looked over the banister to the main foyer.

The open space was illuminated by moonlight coming in from the large glass windows above the front door. But there was another light. She walked downstairs and saw a soft glow coming from inside the office. The door was open. She walked over and saw Mikhail sitting at his desk. His head was down, but she knew he wasn't asleep. She stood there a moment just watching him.

A single lamp shone down on his desk. His laptop was on, and the monitor's blue shadowy radiance cast a soft glow across his face. Both elbows on the armrests, he just sat there.

Nothing had prepared her for meeting him. And the day he walked into her life had changed everything. She'd always known she wanted to have a child. But it wasn't until Derek died and Mikhail came to her that she knew who she wanted the father to be. It was like divine fate had brought him to her that day. And as soon as she'd seen him standing in her doorway, she'd known he was the one. And now she was even surer than ever.

"Hey."

Mikhail looked up at Cyanna standing in the office doorway. He smiled and sat back. "Hey, yourself."

"May I?"

"Sure, of course. Come on in."

She walked farther into the office and looked around. She'd seen it earlier, but at night, in the wee hours of the morning, it looked much different. It looked lonely. He looked lonely.

She knew he watched her as she walked around. She could feel the deep penetration of his eyes on her body. She turned to him and smiled. He nodded.

"Come here," he said.

She raked her teeth over her lower lip. "I think you like ordering me around."

He chuckled softly. "Yeah, I do."

"Thought so," she said, standing her ground. But the seductive twinkle in his eyes soon weakened her resolve. A few seconds later she walked over to where he sat and slowly turned his chair around to face her. She sat down on his desk in front of him. He sat up, pulled the tie and opened the silk robe. He looked down at her naked body and smiled openly.

He leaned in, licked and kissed each nipple. Cyanna sighed, rolling her head back and bracing her hands on the desk. He licked her again and suckled. He was hungry, and her body fed him completely. His kisses burned her skin with near-mindless intensity. In mad passion they devoured each other. Mikhail stood. He abandoned restraint, released the drawstring on his pants and let them drop to the floor. His arousal stood straight at her core. He raised her hips from the desk and entered her in one smooth sealing motion.

She gasped and shrieked until his powerful kiss covered her mouth. Her arms circled his neck, and her legs wrapped securely around his waist. She held tight as he pushed into her over and over again, filling her body completely with each vigorous thrust. They looked into each other's eyes as their rapture neared. Seeing him seeing her was more sensual and erotic than she ever imagined.

Then an instant later their desire exploded. Their bodies tensed rigidly as spikes of ecstasy held them, then slowly released. Breathless, he picked her up and cradled her as he sat back down in his chair. Soothing kisses covered her neck and shoulder. He wasn't done touching her, and she wasn't done wanting him. They went back upstairs. The dance of love continued until the early hours of dawn.

Chapter 7

The next few days went by quickly in an exciting blur of joyful entertainment and sensual pleasure. Cyanna and Mikhail spent most of the time together talking, getting to know each other and enjoying the intimate pleasures of their newly forged pact. Later, Mikhail took her out and around to see the wondrous sights of Key West. She saw his world through his eyes, and she loved it.

At first they visited the usual tourist locations, but then he took her to his favorite places on the island and beyond.

At the end of the week Cyanna woke up to a gentle kiss on the back of her shoulder. She moaned sleepily, then exhaled her exhilarated joy. The past few days she'd been living a fantasy on cloud nine. Mikhail was amazing. Each morning they'd wake up late and naked, wrapped in each other's arms. They'd make love in the tub or shower stall. They'd eat, relax, talk, read, swim, then retire to the secluded backyard getaway and make love all over again. At night they'd lie out beneath the stars and enjoy each other's bodies until the early-morning dawn.

As a lover he was without equal. He was loving, tender, spontaneous, confident, attentive, creative and extremely generous. Just thinking about what he'd done to her body the past few days made her stomach shudder with excited delight. Every time he looked at her, she wanted him all over again.

Every care, every desire, every need and every want had been thoroughly and completely fulfilled by him. He had cherished her mind, her body and her spirit. Being with him had exceeded all her desires. She had never been so elated. She smiled to herself. He was right—this was so much better than a sterile room in a fertility clinic.

A second kiss came; this time he moved her hair aside and added a sweet nuzzle to her neck as he pulled the top sheet away from her body. He massaged her neck and shoulders, then stroked the length of her back and caressed her buttocks. She smiled again, loving the feel of his hands on her body.

He leaned in and kissed her ear. "Good morning," he whispered.

"Good morning," she hummed.

"How'd you sleep?" he asked, continuing to kiss her earlobe.

She giggled at his tickling tongue and tender kisses.

"Great," she said, rolling over to the side and looking up at Mikhail. He was wearing jeans and a T-shirt. "You're dressed. Are we going out this morning?"

"I am. I need to take care of a few things at the marina. It'll probably take a good part of the day."

"Aw," she moaned, commiserating. "Back to work. Reality looms already."

He smiled and nodded while gently stroking the length of her body. "Yep, already, but I'll be back later this afternoon."

"Can I come?"

He smiled mischievously. "You want to come?" he asked.

She nodded.

"Are you sure?" he asked.

She nodded again.

"Okay," he said and began pulling the sheet down from her body. His eyes immediately focused on her pert breasts, dark areola and soft nipples. "Ah yes, now this is what I call the perfect morning delight." He leaned down and nibbled and licked her nipples until they were as hard as diamonds. She gasped and sighed. His hot breath made her body burn and her blood sizzle. He opened his mouth and took her in. Panting gently, she cradled his head, moaning at the sensuous sucking. His hand reached down to her thighs and then came up between her legs.

She giggled and squirmed away from him, rolling to the other side of the bed. He reached for her again, but she blocked his hands. "That's not the kind of coming I was talking about," she playfully scolded.

"Really? Are you sure?" he said.

"You know that's not what I meant," she said.

"Come here," he said. She shifted closer. He kissed her lovingly. "I'll be back in a few hours." He stood and turned to leave.

"Promise?" she said, watching him go.

He turned and nodded. "Stay right there. Get some rest. I'll join you soon."

She raked her teeth over her lower lip and smiled as her stomach fluttered. The look in his eyes told her he had all intentions of spending the rest of the day in her arms. She lay back down, listening to his footsteps as he walked down the steps. Shortly afterward she heard the front door open and close. She got up and headed to the bathroom.

She showered and dressed and then went down to the kitchen to get something to eat. As soon as she reached the foyer, the front doorbell rang. An overnight deliveryman was standing there with three extra-large boxes addressed to her. She knew these were the things she'd asked Donna to send. She signed for them, and he brought them inside. As soon as he left, she opened the first two boxes, delighted that her clothes had finally arrived.

She turned her attention to the third box, labeled Fragile. More lightweight than the other two, she opened it and saw the exorbitant amount of foam peanuts and padding on top. Without going farther, she knew exactly what it was. She hadn't asked Donna to send it, but here it was. She knew this was her practice instrument without removing a single peanut.

She pulled it out, fingered the bow and strings, then placed it on the foyer table and turned her attention to the clothes. She took the first two boxes upstairs and looked through her selection. Although suitable and comfortable, the outfits were far more practical and businesslike than she'd expected. She really didn't own any casual lightweight clothing. Disappointed, she shook her head, realizing she'd have to get some new things sooner rather than later. But right now she had a call to make.

"This is Donna Van Kelp."

"Hey, Donna, it's me. I just received the boxes. Thank you."

"Sure, no problem. I hope everything arrived in one piece."

"Yes, everything's just fine. By one piece I presume you mean my violin."

"Okay, I know. I know. But I couldn't resist and you know I can't mind my own business. I was standing in your bedroom packing your clothes and I saw the instrument sitting there on the stand. And like I said, I couldn't resist. I had to send it. I'm not going to let you walk away and just give up on your talent."

"I know and I'm not," Cyanna said. "And thank you."

"You're welcome. Also I got a call from your friend in Qatar. He still wants you back, or rather his grandfather does."

Cyanna sighed heavily. "When?" she asked.

"Yesterday, today, right now, as soon as possible. Apparently his grandfather is asking for you constantly. I told him you weren't in town, but he insisted he'd send his jet to pick you up wherever you are."

Cyanna looked around and shook her head. "No, I can't. I need to do this."

"And the money?" Donna asked.

"I need to do this," Cyanna repeated.

"All right, as long as you're sure," Donna said.

Cyanna nodded, affirming her position. "Yes, I'm positive."

"Okay, I'll take care of it. So, how's everything going down there?"

"Great, fantastic, couldn't be more wonderful," Cyanna said, smiling and thinking of Mikhail. "Mikhail is an amazing man. Hopefully this time next month I'll be headed back home with a little something extra tucked away."

"Cyanna, can you really walk away just like that?" Donna asked quietly.

Cyanna stopped smiling. She paused a moment before answering her friend. She knew she wouldn't have a choice. As soon as she was pregnant she needed to move on and get back to her life. "Yes," she said softly. "I can. I have to."

"Okay, Twitter me, text me, keep me posted."

"I will. Take care."

She ended the call and looked around at her clothes scattered on the bed. She gathered them up and began hanging them in the closet and putting them in the drawers. Just as she finished, she heard the front door open and voices calling out for Mikhail. She stopped and looked around. They were female voices. She walked out of the bedroom and over to the stairs and peered over the banister. There was no one in the foyer, but she heard talking and laughter coming from the kitchen area. She called out, "Hello? Can I help you?"

Two women walked back to the foyer and looked up the stairs. Neither spoke. They looked at each other and then back to her.

"Mikhail's not here. May I help you with something?"

"And you are?" one of the women asked sternly.

Cyanna started walking down the stairs slowly. "I'm a friend of Mikhail's. And you are?"

They looked at each other again, smiled and then turned back to Cyanna. "I'm Tatiana," one answered.

"I'm Natalia," the other added. "We're his sisters."

Cyanna smiled and walked down the rest of the steps quicker. "Tatiana, Natalia, hi. It's a pleasure to meet you both and finally put a face to the stories. I've heard so much about you. Mikhail talks about you and Nikita all the time. I'm Cyanna, a friend of his." She shook each sister's hand happily.

"Sorry for just letting ourselves in like this. We wouldn't have just walked in had we known someone was here. Unfortunately, Mikhail didn't mention the house was currently rented."

"It's not rented. I'm kind of staying here with him for a while."

"How long is a while?" Tatiana asked with her usual journalistic inquisitiveness.

"Actually we're not sure yet. We have an understanding of sorts," she added, purposely trying not to say too much.

"What kind of an understanding of sorts?" Tatiana continued questioning suspiciously.

"It's a personal arrangement," Cyanna answered vaguely.

"Okay," Natalia said. "Do you know where he is?"

"Yes, he's down at the marina this morning. I expect him later. If you'd like to come back or leave a message…"

"No, that's okay. We'll head down there and catch up with him. Thanks. It was nice meeting you, Cyanna."

"You, too," Cyanna said.

The sisters looked at each other, nodded and headed to the front door. Just as they opened it, Cyanna called to them.

"Um, maybe you can help me," she began. They turned around. "I need to buy some clothes more suitable to this climate. Can you suggest a few places I can shop in town?"

"Sure," Tatiana said.

"Actually, we were headed out to a few boutiques ourselves. You're welcome to join us, if you'd like."

"Sure," Natalia chimed in, adding a nod to the invitation.

Cyanna smiled. "Are you sure? I wouldn't want to impose."

"No, not at all. Please, we insist. We're having a girls' day out—lunch, shopping and gossip. Join us. It'll be fun. We can hear some of those stories our brother's been telling you."

Cyanna smiled. "Great. I'll grab my purse and be right out."

A few minutes later Cyanna got into Natalia's backseat. "Thank you so much."

"Not at all, it's our pleasure," Tatiana said. "Since you're obviously a good friend of our brother's, this is the perfect way to get to know you." She paused briefly as Natalia pulled out of the driveway and headed into town. "So, where are you from?"

"I live in New York City."

"Cool. What do you do there?" Natalia asked, looking up in the rearview mirror.

"I'm a classical musician. I play the violin."

"Wait, are you Cyanna Dupres?" Tatiana turned and asked.

"Yes, I am."

"I know you. Or rather I know your work," Natalia said. "I love it. I play your performances all the time, especially in the Teen Center. Your music relaxes me and really helps me concentrate and focus, and it introduces the teens to another form of music. Hey, maybe we can arrange for you to come and talk to the kids. I know they'd love to meet you."

"That sounds like fun. I'd like that."

"Oh yeah, I enjoy your work, as well. You are very talented," Tatiana added. Natalia nodded in agreement. "So," Tatiana began again after a short pause. "You and our brother are friends." Cyanna nodded. "Have you known him long?"

"A little while," Cyanna said, circumventing their curiosity.

"Good friends, as in seeing each other romantically?" Tatiana hinted for more clarified information.

"It's a bit more complicated than that," Cyanna hedged.

"What do you mean complicated?" Natalia asked as she parked.

"Ah, I think I'd better let Mikhail tell you when he's ready."

Tatiana looked at Natalia. They knew for certain something was up now. They just had no idea what it was. And, knowing their brother, he'd never tell them. Getting it from Cyanna was their only hope.

Their first stop was to Nikita's Café for a quick breakfast snack. Over beignets and lattes they talked and joked about Cyanna's music experiences, Tatiana's strangest interviews and Natalia's high-spirited sons, Brice and Jayden. Afterward they headed to a popular local boutique. They went in and were immediately welcomed by their friend and the store's owner. The sisters helped Cyanna pick a few stylish outfits, then Cyanna and Natalia assisted Tatiana in choosing a dress for a red-carpet music affair later that week.

They shopped at a few more boutiques, then continued to another larger store, where they bought several more summer outfits. Their last stop was a children's boutique, where Natalia and Tatiana found a number of seasonal outfits for Brice and Jayden. While the sisters stood in line to pay for their purchases, Cyanna waited and browsed, wandering around the store.

After paying, Tatiana looked around. "Hey, where did Cyanna go?" she asked.

"I don't know. She was right here a few minutes ago." They started walking around the immediate area; then Natalia entered the baby's department. "There she is, over by the display."

Tatiana walked over, looked around and saw Cyanna standing at a display holding a tiny Onesie and admiring a pair of knitted baby booties.

Natalia turned to her sister and whispered questioningly, "Baby booties and a Onesie?"

Tatiana shrugged and nodded. "Uh-huh, that's what it looks like to me."

Cyanna turned, seeing the sisters and smiling awkwardly. "Hey, are you guys ready?" she asked as she put the booties and Onesie back on the rack. "Um, I was just looking at the baby things," she said.

"Are you—" Natalia asked.

"Me? Oh no," Cyanna said. "It's just that I can never resist baby things. They're so tiny and so precious." She paused, sighed and repeated, "No."

"Sounds like your biological clock is ticking," Tatiana said.

"I guess it is. I love babies and children."

"You should have some."

"I hope so. Maybe one day," she said wistfully. "Ready?"

"Yes, it does sound like you're ready," Tatiana observed.

"You know you can always go to an in vitro specialist. I did and I have two incredible sons to show for it," Natalia said.

They talked about Natalia's experience as they

walked out of the store and continued shopping. An hour later, after stopping at a food market and then for take-home dessert from the café, Natalia and Tatiana dropped Cyanna off at Mikhail's house.

Twenty minutes later, Natalia and Tatiana were parked at the marina. They walked along the long private dock to one of their brother's boats.

"Hey up there," Natalia called, raising her hand to block the bright sun from her eyes.

Mikhail looked over the rail at his sisters standing on the dock. They waved.

"Hey, I didn't know you guys were coming by today. I'll be right down." He finished wrapping up a rope, then jumped down from the boat. "What's up?" he asked.

"You tell us," Tatiana said. Natalia grinned.

"What do you mean?" he asked after hugging them.

"You're not hiding or protecting her or you never would have left her alone in the house...." Tatiana began.

"Plus we would have never met her," Natalia added.

Tatiana nodded. "You don't usually have traditional relationships, so we can eliminate the 'I've fallen in love and she's living with me now' scenario."

"And with everything I've read about her, she's not likely to be a one-night-stand type. So, what's the deal with you and Cyanna Dupres?" Natalia asked, ending their deductive reasoning.

Mikhail smiled. "You stopped at the house?"

They nodded. "Oh, we did more than that," Natalia hinted.

"What do you mean you did more than that?" he asked.

"What's going on, Mikhail? Why is Cyanna Dupres staying at your house? And we know it's not business or we'd never ask."

"She's a friend," he said.

"Yeah, we got that part from her. What else?"

"She's visiting the area," he said, watching Fannie hurrying down the dock toward them. She waved at him. He knew he was needed in the main office.

"And…" Tatiana prompted.

"And she needed a place to stay, so I—"

"Mikhail," Fannie called out. "Got a minute? We need you."

"Sure. I'll be right there," he told Fannie. She nodded, turned and walked back down the dock. "Sorry, ladies, duty calls." He smiled at his sisters. "I'll check in with you later." He hugged them again and strolled down the dock.

"Not funny, Mikhail," Natalia called out after him.

He waved and kept walking. Natalia and Tatiana looked at each other and shook their heads. "You know, if I didn't know any better, I'd say he planned that," Tatiana said.

"I know better, and he probably did," Natalia said as they headed back to the car and drove home.

Chapter 8

Mikhail knew his sisters well. Once they had a taste of curiosity, there was no way they were going to just give up on being interested about Cyanna's presence in his home, especially Tatiana.

As soon as he walked in the front door, he smelled something cooking and heard salsa music playing. He headed to the kitchen, but hesitated when he saw the overnight delivery package containing the violin and bow on the foyer table. He picked it up and examined it. It was much smaller than he'd expected. He plucked one of the strings, listening to the sound reverberate within the wooden instrument. He put it back down and continued to the kitchen.

He paused in the doorway, watching Cyanna sway and gyrate her hips as she peering into a large pot on the stove. She was dressed in a colorful floor-length body-hugging halter dress. She looked stunning, sexy and undeniably inviting.

The thin ribbon tied in a bow behind her neck tempted him to release it. He licked his lips as his fingers itched at the thought of pulling her dress away and thrusting into her over and over again until their bodies tensed and exploded in unrestrained passion. The desire to make love to her right there on the kitchen table sent a rush of excitement through his veins directly to his groin. A familiar firm tightness pulled at the front of his jeans.

She had a way of affecting him like that. His breath quickened, and his body tensed. He wanted her all the time, and right now he wasn't sure this feeling was ever going to stop. He was getting very used to coming home and having her there waiting for him. After everything he'd done in his life, this was what he'd always wanted. Peace and serenity at the end of the day with a woman in his arms. But not just any woman—he wanted Cyanna. The truth in his words echoed in his heart and mind. Yes, he wanted her.

He'd known the moment she'd opened her apartment door months ago that she would be important to him. It wasn't until later that weekend that he'd realized how important. But she wasn't ready for him after so soon losing Derek. That's why he'd had to walk away before she got too attached. He'd done it once. Could he do it again? Could he really end this when the time came to walk away with her carrying his child? He shook his head slowly, mentally answering his own question. No, having a child could be the beginning of a new life for both of them.

"Hey," he said, leaving his thoughts and walking over to the stove to greet her.

Cyanna turned, smiling, then put the wooden spoon she'd been stirring with on the dish beside the burner. "Hey. I didn't hear you come in. But, as usual, perfect timing."

"Actually I have to get back to the marina shortly. I'm expecting a very special delivery. But I thought I'd take a break and come home for a quick snack," he said, wrapping his arms around her waist while moving his body with hers to match the rhythmic salsa music. "Umm, delicious."

"That would be dinner. I thought I'd cook for you tonight."

"Yes, what you're cooking smells delicious, but I wasn't talking about the food. I was talking about you. You look mouthwatering, and I'm a starving man."

"Well, starving man will have to wait a few more minutes," she said, playfully pushing back against him with her rear.

"Ah yes, do that again," he joked.

"You're incorrigible." She chuckled and pushed back more slowly this time.

"Yes, I am, but only for you. So, what's cooking?" He reached around her and tipped the lid on a small pot of steaming rice. Then he reached to look into the larger pot as she moved to the side counter.

"It's seafood gumbo, my own special recipe. It'll be ready in about fifteen minutes, but it's even better when it's heated up later this evening. I just have to add the shrimp, lump crabmeat and the last few ingredients." She began chopping a small bunch of flat leaf parsley.

Mikhail grabbed a spoon from the drawer and tasted the steaming-hot brew. "Mmm, this is good. Spicy, exactly how I like it."

"Me, too. Oh, do you have any filé powder?"

"Yeah, I think so," he said, checking his seasoning cabinet, then pulling down a small glass jar from the top shelf. He placed it on the counter beside her. "Need any help?" he asked.

"No, I'm good," she said.

"And tasty," he muttered as he kissed and nibbled the sweet curve of her neck and pressed his body close. The music slowed to a more sultry, seductive melody, and his body slowed to the new rhythm. He kissed her neck again, and she turned within his embrace and their lips locked instantly. The kiss was ravenous, sweeping them both up in its consuming intensity. When his mouth pulled from hers, she gasped breathlessly.

"Stove, pot, I need to turn it off," she muttered.

He nodded, and reaching over, he turned off the burner and slid the pot aside. In one smooth move he stepped away from the stove and pressed her against the counter. He held her tight, and his mouth and hands were all over her body. She loved it. "I've been thinking about you lying in bed waiting for me all day," he murmured as a deep guttural groan rumbled from his throat. "Do you have any idea how much I want and need you right now?"

Her body reeled from his confession. They kissed

again, and the rage of passion exploded. He released the bow behind her neck and pulled the front of her dress down. Her breasts stood pert and waiting with her nipples already hard for him. He gazed at his treasure with ardent approval. He licked his lips, then tasted one and then the other. He suckled, and her head rolled back as she gasped and panted. His mouth and tongue were deliciously thorough, and she wanted everything he gave.

Unable to take much more, she pulled back. He looked into her eyes. She reached down, feeling the thick bulge between his legs, and her wetness flowed freely. She stroked and rubbed the full length of him as his eyes seared into hers. She moved to unzip his pants and felt a vibration in his pocket. "Your phone," she said.

"What phone?"

"In your pocket, it's ringing."

"It's work. Forget it," he said.

"Are you sure?" she asked.

"Answer a phone right now, when I have you in my arms, are you kidding me?" he said as he nibbled her neck.

She smiled, pleased by his answer. "But what if it's important?" she whispered in his ear and then kissed his neck.

"Then they'll call back." The vibrations in his pocket stopped. "See, it stopped, not important." An instant later the house phone began ringing.

"I think they just called back, and that would make it important." She leaned back. "Looks like it's gonna be work first, darling. We have plenty of time tonight."

His cell phone vibrated again. "Answer the phone." She smiled and went back to the stove to resume cooking.

Mikhail answered and had a brief discussion with the person on the other end. Even though her back was turned, it was impossible for Cyanna not to overhear his side of the conversation.

"Hey, did she get there yet?…Okay. How long?…No, I'll take care of that when I get there…Nah, go, I'll be back later." He glanced at his watch, agreed to something else and finally ended the call and came back to stand behind her at the stove.

It was obvious that the nice romantic dinner Cyanna had planned was overshadowed by whoever "she" was. "I guess you have to get back to the marina now," she stated.

"Later," he said, tasting the food again. "So, how was your day?"

"Interesting, you had a couple of visitors earlier," she said.

"Yes, I know. Tatiana and Natalia stopped by the marina."

She smiled. "Your sisters are really cool."

Mikhail chuckled. "Yes, they are."

"We talked, we laughed and we shopped most of the day."

He nodded. "I presume they wanted to know who you are and why you're here with me."

"Yes, they did, repeatedly."

He smiled. "And you wouldn't tell them."

"No, I wouldn't."

He chuckled. "Good. But of course that's not the end of it."

"I didn't think it would be." She stopped stirring and looked up at him. "Are you going to tell them about us, what we're really doing, trying to do?"

"Our arrangement," he noted. "No."

She nodded slowly, suddenly feeling a hollow emptiness in the pit of her stomach. The fact that he had no intention of telling his sisters and probably the rest of his family about her and their hoped-to-be child hurt her more than she'd thought it would. It was suddenly painfully obvious that neither she nor her child would be welcome as legitimate members of the Coles family. "I get it. You don't think they would understand."

"Actually, they would understand. More than you know, particularly Natalia."

"But what we're doing is very different."

He nodded. "Yes, it is, but the same end results."

She turned and went back to stirring the gumbo. "And you still won't tell them."

"No."

She stopped and released the spoon.

"Having second thoughts?" he asked her.

"No, no, of course not, I want this child, my child, very much. I just… I guess I hoped…" She stopped and took a deep breath. "Never mind."

"No, tell me. What is it?"

She shook her head. "It's nothing. Why don't you get back to the marina and do what you have to do. The sooner you get there, the sooner you'll be back."

He nodded. "Okay. I don't know how long this is going to take. I'll be back as soon as I can."

"I'll be here." She turned and watched as he left the kitchen. As soon as she heard the front door close, she turned everything off and sat down, cupping her chin. She took a deep breath, releasing it slowly. She should have stuck to her original plan and insisted that Mikhail go to the in vitro clinic. She knew that if she didn't step back she was going to be in for a lot of heartache. As soon as he got her pregnant, she'd walk away.

"That's it, no more feelings, no more emotions and definitely no more pity party," she vowed, disregarding her heart. "This is business, just business."

The door opened and closed again. Cyanna looked up at Mikhail walking back into the kitchen. "You're back."

He nodded. "I'm back." He walked over to her and put his hand out. She took it and stood.

"I thought you needed to be at the marina."

He shook his head. "No. I'm exactly where I need to be right now, with you."

Cyanna smiled. How could a man make her feel so good and know exactly what to do and say to melt her heart? "Let's eat."

Cyanna finished making the gumbo while Mikhail cleaned up and set the table on the patio. They sat out and ate, relishing the comfort of each other's company and the ease of conversation. Afterward they cleaned up and Mikhail loaded the dishwasher. Cyanna went back outside into the yard while he finished. Whoever *she* was and whatever he needed to do with her seemed to have completely faded away. As far as Cyanna was concerned, in his eyes tonight, she was the only woman on the planet, and she loved that feeling.

She stood, thinking about getting pregnant. The joy she felt filled her heart. She stepped out farther and looked up at the brilliant sky filled with stars. There were so many, and they were so breathtakingly beautiful. She'd never seen them so stunning. When she traveled she never took the time to look up and appreciate their beauty, and when she was home the city lights of New York drowned and obscured their radiance. So this was a rare treat. She looked down, stroked her stomach and smiled, thinking about showing her child all this beauty for the first time.

"Soon."

She turned to Mikhail behind her. She nodded and looked back up at the sky as if to make a silent wish. "You know, it really is so beautiful here. It's perfect serenity."

"Yes, it is. So, tell me, you're on leave right now," he said, moving beside her. She nodded. "And how exactly does that work? Do you just stop playing for a while?"

"Yes, something like that. I finished my performance tour schedule three weeks ago and I don't have to go into the studio for another few months. That means I'm completely free except for a few personal performances and a few I usually give for a very special fan."

"A very special fan?" Mikhail queried.

She nodded. "Yes, he flies me in for a couple private performances. I stay a few days, hanging out, and then I go back home. I've cancelled them for the time being."

"Should I be jealous?"

She chuckled. "No, I don't think so. Aziz Robah is close to eighty years old. He's a very sweet, very old man who smiles when he sees me. He played violin when he was younger, and he enjoys listening to my music."

"I don't presume he makes the travel arrangements for you."

"No, his grandson makes the arrangements. They have a private jet, actually several private jets. Ammar comes and picks me up personally. They live in Dawlat, Qatar. It's a small nation close to—"

Mikhail nodded tightly. "I know Qatar. So this fan and his grandson, Ammar, they must be very wealthy to fly you in special every year just to perform."

"Actually it's more like every few months. They have means."

"So you just go over there and perform for Aziz?" he said.

"Well, the rest of the immediate family is there, as well."

"Which includes the grandson no doubt," he said. "And then what happens?"

Even in the soft veranda lighting, she saw the tight grimace cross his face. She sighed, knowing where this was going. It was the same line of questioning she'd gotten from her brother years ago. She began walking down the narrow path to the cabana. Landscape lighting illuminated as she walked. He followed. "Then I usually spend a few days hanging with the family, shopping or just touring around the country. It's a very modern and beautiful region, and their home, a palace, is extremely serene. I'm respectful of their country's culture and traditions and also they pay me extremely well. And Aziz has a small crush on me."

"It sounds more like the grandson has the crush, not the grandfather. Let me guess, Ammar personally escorts you around the country, first-class everything, impressive lunches, exotic dinners and so on." She nodded. "And he is always very respectful."

"Yes, of course. What's the big deal? It's just a gig."

"No, it's a personal gig. It's very different. Perhaps you should consider getting another gig elsewhere. That region of the world isn't exactly stable at the moment."

"Yes, Qatar is in the Persian Gulf, but as I'm sure you're well aware, Qatar has strong military ties with the United States and has a very solid U.S. presence."

"You still need to drop them," he said.

"Are you presuming to run my life again?" she asked.

He held his hands up in playful surrender. "Just a suggestion," he offered.

"Duly noted," she said, smiling tightly.

"So, will you play for me?" he asked. She looked away. "What?"

She took a deep breath. "Actually, my playing has been off."

"What do you mean?"

She shook her head. "It's off, it's wrong, it's gone. I can't play anymore," she said softly. "I've lost it."

He took her hands in his and kissed each finger lovingly and then the palms of her hands. "No, you haven't. It's there inside of you. You're incredibly talented. Whatever you feel you've lost is still right there inside of you."

She nodded. "I hope so."

He pulled her into his embrace. She laid her head against his chest and relaxed in his comforting strength. They stood in silence as the brilliance of twilight beamed down and the flicker of candlelight behind them faded.

They walked to what was now her cabana. She sat down on the chaise and lay back, looking up. He went to release the side drapes.

"No, leave them open," she said. "No one's here but us." He nodded and pulled the ceiling drape back, revealing the stars above. He lay down beside her while releasing the clamp. The chaise began to gently swing. Cyanna looked up and smiled. The stars shone brightly above them. "Wow," she whispered as he held her tight. She snuggled into his embrace.

"Was the grandson, Ammar, the other man you considered?"

"Yes," she said quietly. "But I'm glad you agreed."

"You realize, of course, you're not going back there. Ever."

She chuckled. "You just can't help yourself, can you?"

"Consider it an addendum to the second condition."

"Sorry, it's much too late to add addendums. And speaking of which, you never told me the third condition," she said.

"I will later," he said, kissing her forehead. "So what are your plans for tomorrow?"

"I don't know yet. What do you do around here for fun?"

"Sail, swim, snorkel, shop…"

"I get it, anything that begins with the letter *S*."

"No, but this is Key West, the party town of the States. We have everything here, including a dozen festivals a week."

"Oh right, Natalia and Tatiana were talking about a few of the festivals this week. They mentioned one called the Midnight Madness Festival. It's tonight, right? And it's private and it sounded really fun and interesting. Do you know about it?"

"Yes, I know about it."

"Is it in town?"

"Not exactly," he said. "It's more private than public."

"So what kind of festival is it?"

"It's hard to explain."

She sat up and looked down at him. "Well, what happens there?"

He took a deep breath and sighed. "It's more of you have to see it to believe it kind of thing."

"Fine, let's go see it. Is it far?" she asked.

He smiled. "Actually, it's by invitation only."

She looked at him slyly. "Can you get us an invitation?"

"I already have one."

"Well, good. Let's go then. I probably need to change and find something nicer to wear." She got off the chaise.

He sat up. "That won't be a problem. It's a clothing-optional festival. It takes place on a private beach at the end of an outlet and at the stroke of twelve all clothes come off. It's mandatory. That's why it's called Midnight Madness."

Her jaw dropped, and she blushed. "I'm guessing you've gone a time or two."

"A time or two." He winked.

"Okay, I think I'll pass. To tell you the truth, I think I'd rather just sit here and look up at all the stars. It's absolutely amazing to see the sky lit up like this."

Mikhail got off the chaise. "Come on. I have an idea."

"Does it involve removing my clothes in public?" she asked.

"Only in private and only for me, but you will see stars, a lot of them," he assured her. "You'll love it, I promise."

They got into his car and drove to the marina. It was dark and the place seemed deserted, but she heard music coming from one of the yachts moored on the dock. They walked down the familiar platform to the end boat.

The boat drifted on the waves; then he started it up, turned on the running lights and steered it out of the marina. Cyanna stood behind him, watching everything he was doing. She was amazed at how proficient he was.

Now, on the open sea, she was surprised that there were so many boats out so late at night.

"What do all the colored lights mean?"

"They're the rules of the road. It's nighttime etiquette. White lights on the stern, that's the back of the boat. The green lights are on the starboard and red on the port. It's all about who's the give-way vessel."

"So where are we going?"

"To a wildlife reserve."

"Isn't something like that off-limits?" she asked.

"We'll be fine."

He continued out into the darkness for about fifteen minutes. Then he seemed to steer the boat in a large circle with bright lights beaming out in every direction. He slowed.

"Why did you do that?" she asked.

"I needed to make sure no other boats were around." He cut the motor, and there was silence except for the lapping of gentle waves on the boat's hull. He dimmed the boat's bright lighting. "Come on—let's go down on deck. You'll see better," he said.

They stood in the center of the deck. "Are you ready?" he asked. "Close your eyes." She did.

He turned all the boat lights off. Mikhail stood behind her. "Open."

Cyanna opened her eyes and gasped as she slowly looked around her. The sky sparkled and shone. Brilliant stars surrounded them above and reflected on the surface of the water below. In the total darkness, they were completely surrounded by the radiant infinity of the heavens.

"Oh my God, this is amazing," she whispered in sheer astonishment. "What—what is this place?"

"We're out in the middle of nowhere and far enough away from Key West and the ambient lights of the city."

She giggled, stunned by everything she saw. "It's

incredible. It's like drifting in space. I've never seen anything so magnificent," she muttered softly. "Thank you for bringing me here. I never imagined such awesome beauty."

"I'd say this was much better than the Midnight Madness Festival," he said in her ear as he loosened the tie around her neck and pulled her dress zipper down. The dress slipped to her hips, falling to the deck. He massaged her shoulders and her back. He cupped her breasts and massaged them as his thumbs stroked her nipples. His hands roamed all over her body. He pulled the elastic band down and slipped his hand between her legs.

She moaned, knowing her panties were already drenched. She gasped loudly as his finger dipped inside of her and began tantalizing her already swollen nub. Her hips began to move of their own volition. Her legs weakened, and she stumbled back into him. He guided her to sit down. She did, but all she could see was his shadow and the surrounding stars.

"I can't see you," she whispered breathlessly.

"You don't have to, just feel me."

"You still have your clothes on."

"This isn't about us making a baby right now. It's about your pleasure, and I've been needing to taste you again. It's been way too long, and I'm a starving man."

Her thoughts spun wildly. She knew exactly what he meant. She remembered he'd done it before in her apartment. Her stomach clenched and quivered. Her hands trembled. Her breath halted as she sat.

He removed her panties, then spread her legs and placed each on his shoulders. Yes, she knew exactly what he intended to do. Her breathing increased and her stomach jumped in anticipation. He kissed, licked and nibbled the insides of her thighs. She trembled in eagerness. The warmth of his breath seared her skin and made her body tingle. She closed her eyes and held tight to the edge of the boat. Her breathing stuttered and her gasps got louder. The starving man began to eat.

He licked her core with the flat of his tongue. Her body quaked and her legs trembled to close, but she couldn't. He was there, right where she needed him. Her ragged breathing seemed to spur him on. His tongue stiffened and spread her lips. She gasped as he entered her. She squirmed and moaned as his mouth widened to devour all of her. He was slow, gentle and thorough. He feasted like he had all the time in the world. After several minutes, hours, days, of sheer madness he took the nib of her pleasure into his mouth and suckled.

She screamed her mindless pleasure instantly. His vigorous action increased. Sucking, licking, teasing her more robustly. The more she squirmed and moaned, the more he increased her arousal. Her body shuddered as she panted wildly. Her heart beat faster and faster. She was quickly reaching her point of no return. Seconds later, she screamed her pleasure out again into the place called nowhere.

Over and over again she climaxed in spasms of rapturous ecstasy. She quivered and trembled. Then just as she caught her breath, he started again. Slow to fast, then fast to slow. Her legs opened wider and Mikhail gorged himself on her wetness, licking and devouring her. The wicked, wonderful feel of his mouth in constant hunger spurred her to want more each time and go further. She couldn't stop herself. The freedom of being out in the middle of nowhere, surrounded by the stars with Mikhail between her legs was beyond mind-blowing exhilaration. After one last heart-stopping, body-tensing, nerve-tingling, mind-bending orgasm, she yielded, lying back, completely worn-out.

She closed her eyes as his tender kisses touched her body. His hands and his lips were everywhere all at once. Moments later she opened her eyes, still breathless. She reached out to him, feeling his hardness. She smiled to herself in the sparkling darkness. She stroked the length of him, then unsnapped and unzipped his pants. "Take your clothes off," she said boldly.

"It sounds like you want more," he said.

"Oh yes, much more. I want all of you," she said. He removed his clothes. She lay back and pulled him on top of her. He entered her in one smooth motion. His first thrust was slow and controlled. The second and third increased slightly as he held her tighter and pushed deeper and deeper inside. Then the pace quickened faster and faster. Her breasts bounced, and she held tight to his strong muscled arms. Within moments his pleasure erupted and then hers once more.

They lay naked in each other's arms on the cushioned deck, completely surrounded by stars for what seemed like forever. Without words, they both knew without a doubt, this was more than just making a baby, this was falling in love.

Chapter 9

Three days had passed since their wondrous night on the boat beneath the stars. For her, that night had been the pinnacle of romance. Being in the middle of the ocean surrounded by sparkling stars was like nothing she had ever experienced. It was beyond magical.

Since that time they'd eased into a perfectly comfortable routine with each other. When Mikhail went to work at the marina in the morning, Cyanna stayed around the house, venturing out only once or twice to walk around the grounds, sit out in the veranda or swim in the pool. Late in the afternoon, when he returned, they'd eat an early dinner and spend the evening exploring the wondrous sights of Key West together.

Every day there was something new and different to do. They snorkeled in the reef, toured the area museums, took a boat ride around the island's nature reserves and reveled in the island's outrageous nightlife. Later at night they talked, danced or just relaxed and enjoyed their time together. But whatever they did, the end was the same: they made love. It was perfect.

But this morning started off differently. It was still early when Cyanna woke up. She rolled over and reached out for Mikhail, but he wasn't there. She leaned up and looked around the bedroom. He had obviously left earlier than usual. She lay back in bed for a few minutes, feeling a complete sense of satisfaction. She was happy. No, she was deliriously happy. It had been a long time since she could say that and really mean it. She yawned, stretched and closed her eyes. The sheer joy she felt lulled her right back to an easy, peaceful sleep.

She woke up again. It was much later than she'd expected. What had seemed like just a brief nap was actually two and a half hours. She sat up and looked around. She was still alone. She sneezed. Great, that's all she needed—a cold. She dragged herself out of bed and padded barefoot into the bathroom. After a nice, long, hot shower, she ran through her usual morning routine, including taking her basal body temperature.

To her surprise, her temperature was slightly off. She sneezed again. She went back to the bedroom and sat down on the side of the bed. She sighed. All of a sudden she was exhausted. Maybe she had been overdoing it the past few weeks.

She pulled out and consulted her electronic ovulation calendar. She hadn't checked it in the past couple of days. At that time her hormonal estrogen levels were high and within the optimal parameters for conceiving.

This morning they had leveled off. Her conception time was well over. She looked at the date on the calendar and realized what it was. Somehow in all the excitement of being here, she'd lost track of the date.

A consuming sadness washed over her. It was the anniversary of her parents' death. This was the first year she'd be alone. Since Derek was dead she was the only one left to celebrate their life and mourn their death.

When she went downstairs, the first thing she saw was the violin still sitting on the foyer table. She picked it up and examined it. She tucked it beneath her chin. She picked up the bow. She cradled the neck, positioning her hands on the fingerboard. In one smooth motion she gently touched the hair of the bow to a single string. A single note flowed freely. She adjusted her chin on the chin rest and pulled through the next three strings.

After a while music flowed from her with brilliant ease. She played Mozart's Concerto no. 3, her favorite. The sparkling melody had her fingers tenderly touching as she pulled and pushed the bow grip to dance over the four synthetic strings. When she finished the piece, she stopped, holding the bow in midair. She released a long, even breath, then let the instrument rest on the table. She smiled. It felt good to play again. It felt right.

She went into the kitchen and grabbed a bottle of water. As she drank, her cell phone rang. It was Donna. "Hello," she said softly.

"Hi. I just wanted to call and see how you were doing."

"I'm fine."

"Cyanna, I know what you're doing is important to

you and I know this day is a hard one, but if you want to just pause everything for the next week or so—"

"No, I'm fine. Yes, I am a little sad and—"

"A little?" Donna asked.

"Okay, I'm enormously sad, but this is my life now. I have no choice but to get used to it," Cyanna said. Donna sighed. Cyanna knew something was up. "Spill it."

"What?"

"I know that sound in your voice. What's up?"

"Ammar called again this morning asking for you. He said that he'll be in the States in a few days and wanted to know if you were ready to play for his grandfather."

"No, I can't."

"I told him that," Donna said. "We talked some more and that's when he offered to double the fee."

"Double the fee. What?"

"Yeah, that's exactly what I said. One hundred thousand dollars to play a private concert is crazy, but they have money to burn, literally. That kind of money can go a long way when you're raising a child alone."

Cyanna shook her head slowly. Donna was right. It was a lot of money. Truth be told, she did just fine making the money she made, but having a small cushion only made sense. But that would mean she'd have to leave Key West and Mikhail, putting everything on hold. She couldn't do that. "Donna, please thank Ammar for me, but I'm still going to have to pass on his very generous offer." She paused a few seconds. "Are you disappointed?"

"No, not at all. Yes, it would have been a nice job and commission. But you need to stick to your guns. I'm proud of you."

"Thanks."

"Okay. I'll talk to you later."

"Donna, wait. Thank you for being so supportive," Cyanna began. "And thank you for sending the violin. It sounds perfect."

"You played," Donna asked, surprised.

"Yes, just now. It was good. I think I'm back."

"Honey, ya never left. Call me if you need me."

"I will. Talk to you soon." Cyanna hung up, smiling and feeling much better.

She picked up the violin and bow, went into the living room and began again. She played, and it felt fantastic to feel her music again. She flowed from one piece to another, back to back, she performed a solo concert of Mozart, Antonio Vivaldi, Johann Strauss, Brahms, Bach and—of course her absolute favorite— Beethoven's violin Concerto in D major.

The music poured from her instrument and flowed flawlessly from her heart. Every note was perfection in its pitch and tone. The tempo and melody varied, some fast, some slow.

After hours of playing, she finally stopped, satisfied that she had regained her gift. She placed the instrument back in the box and was just about to close it when she noticed a piece of paper sticking out from the side.

It was sheet music. A solo sonata she had begun composing years ago but never finished. She looked at the notes on the paper, hearing each in her mind.

She picked up the violin with the music sheet and took everything upstairs to the bedroom. She stood in the small sitting room alcove in the master bedroom and played a few notes. Happily, the acoustical sound had near-perfect tone quality. She placed the sheet music on the marble, pulled the French glass doors together and began playing.

Mikhail busied himself away from the house for the next few days. He needed distance, and the marina was the perfect place to get it. He'd been back in Key West for weeks and the last thing he'd been focusing on was work. Even when he did come into the office, his thoughts were always back at his home with Cyanna. Getting up and leaving her was getting harder and harder to do because he knew one day soon it would all be over.

The likelihood of Cyanna being pregnant with his child at this moment was a very real possibility. They had been together for over two weeks, and if her hormonal calculations were correct, he could already have a child. He smiled to himself.

He'd been distracted since his morning had been more than a little challenging. Taking care of overindulged wealthy clients had never bothered him. They paid large sums of money to stay at his marina with no questions asked. Executives, celebrities, politicians and even a couple of royals have paid his considerable fee for private accommodations and complete discretion. When they needed a place to pause from life, his marina was the perfect refuge. As long as they weren't wanted and it wasn't illegal, he welcomed all to stay in complete anonymity, and he, along with his staff, was always available for their needs.

But today he wasn't in the mood to be available and certainly not amiable. He closed himself off from the madness and stayed in his office, sitting at his desk and catching up on long-ignored paperwork. His thoughts wandered often. This wasn't like him. He was dedicated and meticulous with everything he did, particularly when it came to his marina. But lately his focus had been constantly wavering.

After finally filling out the last requisition order form for a few needed engine parts, he hit the key on his keyboard, sending the request to be processed. He took care of the last of the week's accumulated mail. As soon as he tossed the final envelope into his outgoing bin, he stood and walked over to the large windows and looked out at the dock. The view from the marina's office wasn't nearly as awesome as the view from the crow's nest, but he still saw the water.

Mikhail walked back to his desk and went back to his paperwork. An hour later there was a knock at his door.

"Come in," he said.

The door opened. "Yo," his friend Cisco Powel said, looking in. "I'm back."

"Hey, welcome back. That was quick. I expected you'd be away for another few weeks." Mikhail stood and walked over to greet his friend. They shook hands. "How'd the job go?"

"A few weeks, in and out, not bad at all," Cisco said.

Mikhail nodded. "Good, I guess resistance was light."

"Nothing we couldn't handle. It went off like clockwork."

Mikhail nodded. "Excellent." They walked back to the desk and sat down. "When'd you get back?"

"A few days ago," Cisco said. "I had to do the post—now I'm off the clock for a few."

"Sounds good."

"So what's going on around here?" Cisco asked.

"Nothing much, same ol'," Mikhail said. Then he began telling Cisco about the new boat he'd purchased. There was another knock on the door. Jumper ducked his head into the office. "Hey, your new gal just showed up," Jumper said, smiling.

Mikhail glanced behind Jumper. "Cyanna? Where is she, in the front office?"

Jumper looked at Mikhail, then at Cisco and frowned. "Cyanna, huh? Well, I guess that'll do. It's as good a name as any. She's on the trailer in the parking lot—where else would she be?"

Mikhail shook his head. He was becoming completely hopeless. "Yeah, right, of course, never mind," he said, standing and following Jumper back outside. Cisco lagged behind him as they walked to the parking lot.

"So, Cyanna, huh?" Cisco said. "Who is she?"

Mikhail glanced at him pointedly. "She's a friend, and she's none of your business."

Cisco chuckled.

Mikhail turned and glared. "None of your business," he repeated.

Cisco stopped laughing as he shook his head and raised his hands in mock surrender. "All right, all right, I get it. None of my business."

"So, Cyanna, that's what you're calling this one. Right," Jumper said. Cisco started laughing again.

Mikhail turned and scowled at his friend. "I don't know yet, maybe," Mikhail said, redirecting his attention to Jumper.

"You all right today, boss? You seem a little…out of it."

"I'm fine. I just have a lot on my mind today."

"Are you clocking out again?" Jumper asked hesitantly, knowing about his jobs and how he helped out with his old military team.

"No, not for a while," Mikhail said.

"Maybe you just need to get some rest," Cisco piped up.

"Yeah, maybe," Mikhail said.

The three men got to the main parking lot and continued to where the truck was hitched to the trailer and large boat. Fannie was already there checking out the new boat when they walked up.

"Mikhail, this is perfect," Fannie said as they approached. "We get dozens of rental requests for a catamaran. Our younger clientele are gonna love this."

"Yeah, it looks good, beautiful body, excellent form," Mikhail said approvingly as they approached the trailer and boat.

"Well, you know what they say, looks are deceiving,"

Jumper began. "She looks good on the outside, but we need to check under the hood. This model is a beauty, but they need special care. They can be temperamental."

"She'll be the perfect party boat after fishing and sightseeing," Fannie added.

Luther came from around the side and wolf-whistled loudly. "Ah yeah, man, this is it. This is dope. I can just see us out there hitting the waves on this baby. Can you imagine the parties on this thing? Seriously, man, with two cabins, an owner's suite and plenty of comfortable room to kick back, this baby is gonna be dope. Okay, so when are we gonna load her on the slipway and transfer her into the water? I can't wait to take her out."

"Not so fast. Like Jumper said, we're gonna need to check her out first," Mikhail said as he began walking around, looking at the large boat.

Jumper chuckled. "Yep, that's right," he said as he went in the opposite direction, meeting Mikhail at the stern. "The body looks good, but we gotta check the engine to see what we got. I'm almost sure we're gonna need to amp the power and realign the navigation equipment."

Mikhail nodded and turned around. "What do you think?" he asked Cisco and Fannie.

Cisco nodded steadily. "It can work."

Fannie smiled. "I agree. Our younger boat renters are gonna love this one, especially the front netting. I think I'd better order a few replacements now, just in case. Maybe even a thicker braid."

"Okay, let's unload her and see exactly what we have," Mikhail said.

Cisco and Luther nodded as Jumper climbed into the truck's cab and cautiously drove the trailer and catamaran to one of the maintenance and repair slips in back. After they'd secured the boat on the floating dry dock, they began checking it out thoroughly. It wasn't until hours later that they finally walked away satisfied with Mikhail's new acquisition.

The staff headed home, but Mikhail stopped at his private bungalow first. He went up into the crow's nest and stood at the window, looking out across at the panoramic view. First to the seven bungalows tucked amid the private gardens below and then to the serene horizon beyond the trees. He leaned against the window frame.

He'd always found peace when he looked out the window, but today, unexpectedly, the serenity he had always found eluded him. He looked up as the darkening evening sky approached. The first star already shone brightly. It instantly reminded him of Cyanna and the place called nowhere. The memory was intense. Just thinking about her made his body burn. He had no idea how long he stood there thinking about Cyanna and what he wanted. After a while, he leaned away and walked back to his desk.

He sat down and opened his laptop computer, then clicked to a program he used often for his job. It was designed to perform comprehensive and meticulous background checks by the military and would certainly put Cyanna's detective to shame. He typed in a name, Ammar Robah Sharif from Qatar, and started reading the sites.

"See, I told you he'd still be here," Stephen said.

"Yep, you were right," David answered.

"Yo, man, what's up? Where you been?" Spencer asked.

Mikhail looked up, surprised to see his cousin Stephen Morales and his two new brothers-in-law, Spencer Cage and David Montgomery, standing in the doorway of his office. It was as if they'd appeared out of thin air. He smiled, trying to play it off, but the idea that all three men had come into and walked through his house and up to his office without his knowledge showed he was too distracted and maybe losing his perceptive touch.

"Hey," he said, quickly ending his hour-long investigation. The men crossed the room quickly and met in the middle. After hugs and handshakes, the conversation continued. "So what? You guys are hanging out away from the wives tonight? Where's Dominik?"

"He's on shift," Stephen said. "He's putting serious hours in as the medical center's E.R. director. He's gonna catch up with you later."

"So what are you guys doing out?"

"We're celebrating," Stephen said.

"Celebrating what?" Mikhail asked.

Stephen and David looked to Spencer. Spencer smiled proudly. "I'm gonna be a father."

"Whoa, excellent news. Tatiana's pregnant—congratulations!" Mikhail exclaimed, happy for his sister and brother-in-law. They hugged and everyone laughed happily. "Well, now, this deserves a celebration. Come on. Let's get out of here," Mikhail said. After showing the men his latest acquisition, they decided to head over to a friend's popular club. They sat around, laughing and talking about work, family and of course the women in their lives. David and Stephen reminisced about fatherhood and their wives.

"We're headed over to Cutter tomorrow. You and your friend should join us."

"My friend?" Mikhail asked. "What friend?"

Stephen, Spencer and David looked at each other and smiled.

"All right, let's get on with it," Spencer said.

Mikhail looked at him questioningly. "Get on with what?"

"The intervention."

"What intervention?" Mikhail asked. "What's going on?"

"That's the question of the hour—what's going on with you?" Stephen asked. David and Spencer nodded as the three gave Mikhail their full attention.

"What do you mean?" Mikhail asked.

"Cyanna Dupres," Spencer said.

"Mia and Shauna told Nat and Tatiana about you bringing Cyanna to the hospital to meet the baby," Stephen began. "You don't bring women around us, not around your family, ever."

"Then Nat and Tatiana meet Cyanna living in your home a few days later," David added. "Nat's worried. She told me that no woman has ever lived with you in your house before, ever."

"So, what's the deal, bro? You've never mentioned her before, she shows up out of nowhere and she's living in your house," Spencer said.

"They're worried there's a problem and that you might need our help. So here we are," David said.

Mikhail chuckled, then laughed out loud. David, Spencer and Stephen looked at each other. When Mikhail finally calmed down, he shook his head and smiled. "No, my brothers, I'm sure I can handle this alone. But thanks for your concern anyway. I got this."

"Is it another job?" Spencer asked.

"No."

Stephen nodded his head. "We have money."

"A lot of money," David chimed in.

"A whole lot of money," Spencer added.

Mikhail looked at his family's faces and saw their ardent concern. He took a deep breath and nodded. "Thanks, but I'm fine. We're fine—trust me. Cyanna is very important to me and we're working on a project together. I'll let you know more later on."

The three men accepted his word. A few minutes passed, the small celebration-turned-intervention broke up and everyone headed out. Mikhail drove home, pulling up in front of the house twenty minutes later. He turned the engine off and paused. Before he even got out of the car he heard it. It was haunting, poignant and tender with the slightest hint of sadness. Slow and melodic, the music drew him in. It wasn't something from his classical collection; it was different. The more he listened, the more he wasn't sure he liked it. It was just too heartrending.

He walked into the foyer and looked around until he figured out from where the music was coming. He headed up to the bedroom. He stood in the doorway.

Cyanna was standing in the alcove with her eyes closed, gently pulling the bow across the strings. Mikhail was riveted at the sight of her. She wore a free-flowing, floor-length colorful chiffon draping sarong. She was stunning. The beauty of what she was playing paled to the beauty of seeing her standing there.

He felt her vulnerability pour from her soul through her music. The love in his heart poured out. There was no turning back. She had him—all of him—body, mind and spirit.

She finished playing, pulling the bow all the way down and stopping. He applauded softly. She turned abruptly and only half smiled at seeing him standing there. "Hi," she said softly.

"Hello."

She placed the instrument on the small center table. "I didn't know you were home. How long have you been standing there?"

"Awhile. That was beautiful, haunting. Whose is it?"

"You mean the composer?" she asked. He nodded. "It's mine."

"You wrote that?" he asked. She nodded, then bit at her lower lip nervously. "Wow, you are extremely talented."

"Thank you. I wrote it a long time ago."

"It's very sad."

"Yes, it is. I wrote it for my parents. Today," she began then paused and took a deep breath. "Today is the anniversary of their deaths. I guess I was just feeling…" She stopped talking and turned away.

Mikhail quickly walked over and pulled her into his

arms. She went willingly. The solid strength of his body was exactly what she needed. She melted easily into him and closed her eyes. This was all she ever wanted—to be safe, to be wanted and to be loved in the arms of the man she loved. But how did you tell the man you loved that you wanted more than you knew he was willing to give? Her thoughts swirled with sadness—for herself, her parents, for her brother.

"Derek isn't here. He always makes a point of calling me or coming to me on this day. When his helicopter went down, a part of me died with him. I've been standing behind Derek all my life. Even when I'm onstage, he's there with me. And now he's not. His shadow was safe, and now it's gone. I guess maybe that's why I want to have a baby so badly. Right now I'm alone."

"You're not alone, Cyanna."

"I mean family. I have friends and I guess even extended family, but there's no one close to me. No one I can go to or rely on. And now this is the first time I've ever been really alone before. I guess I need to get used to it."

"No, you don't. You have me. I'll always be here for you."

They went back into the bedroom and sat on the large overstuffed double chair beside the fireplace. She laid her head on his chest, and he draped his arms around her shoulders. After a while she closed her eyes and fell asleep. It was the first night they didn't make love.

Chapter 10

Cyanna moaned in the last remnants of sleep and reached out, feeling for the body always at her side. She took a deep breath and opened her eyes. It was still dark in the bedroom, but she could hear the steady sound of rain falling outside. She turned and looked over to Mikhail. He wasn't in bed. She sat up, grabbed her cell phone on the nightstand and checked the time. It was a little after four in the morning. She knew it was way too early for Mikhail to be at the marina. She waited a short while.

"Mikhail?" He didn't answer.

She grabbed her robe and slipped out of bed to find him. He wasn't in the bathroom or out on the balcony. She went downstairs. She peeked in the living room and the office. She headed to the kitchen. She checked the family room, where she noticed the sheer curtains billowing in the warm nighttime breeze. She walked over to the French doors that led to the covered patio and found Mikhail outside, standing just beyond the trellis in the muted light.

Every gorgeous inch of his body was pure sex appeal, and to her extreme pleasure, he had nothing on. He was stunning. Her stomach quivered as her body craved him. She was intoxicated just looking at him.

She slipped outside into the shroud of darkness and walked up behind him. He was staring out at the pouring rain. She reached out and touched his arm. The passionate, charged connection between them was undeniable. He turned his head slightly to acknowledge her presence. "Hey, what are you doing up? You need your rest."

"So do you. Come back to bed," she said softly.

"I'll be there shortly," he promised. "You go back."

She nodded silently, then gently ran her hand up his arm, over his shoulder and slowly down the center of his back. The strong powerful muscles beneath her hands made her fingers itch and her juices flow. The sheer power of his body was exhilarating. His skin was hot, and that made her insides melt like molten lava. This man had a body designed for fantasies, and every time they made love he proved it.

As a lover he was unequal. He was giving, gentle and tender, but she also knew a different Mikhail. One whose power was all-consuming. One who moved her body to mindless extremes of sexual pleasure.

Their first time together had been different than any other time they'd made love. There had been no holding back, no timidity and no reluctance, and right now that's the man she wanted, not the one with the slight hesitation.

"Do you want to hear a secret?" she said playfully.

"Sure, tell me a secret."

"I love touching you," she whispered mischievously as she ran her hand over his back and down to his waist. She spread her fingers wide, touching as much of his body as she could. "It excites me," she said as she continued her lustful perusal. Then she wrapped her arms around him and rested her face on his back. She closed her eyes and kissed him tenderly. Suddenly every decadent, lustful sexual fantasy she'd ever had came to her. Her heart thundered.

"Every inch of your body makes me weak. Did you know that?" she offered softly as she raked her nails down his back, ending by biting her nails into his rear. His body tensed at feeling the pleasurable pain. She did it again, but this time she kissed his arm as she loosened her robe's tie. "I have fantasies about you and me." She inched closer, rubbing her breasts up and down on his back. Her nipples hardened.

He looked to the side. "Fantasies," he repeated.

"Mmm-hmm," she hummed, kissing across his back as she rubbed and massaged his rear. "Oh yes, lots and lots of fantasies," she said as she wrapped her hands around his chest to teasingly tweak and pinch his nipples. He inhaled quickly. She smiled, enjoying the sounds of his strained desire. "Yep, ever since our first night a long time ago. Do you remember the first time we were together?"

"Yes," he muttered as hot, steamy memories surfaced.

"I remember," she whispered over his shoulder. "It was the most powerful and intense night of my life. I know neither of us expected it to happen, but when it did, it was a sexual explosion. We were on the sofa," she said, teasing his nipples. "On the floor—" she pinched them "—on our knees." She scratched down his chest, then went lower. "Against the wall, kissing, grabbing, pushing, pulling, pounding in and out over and over again and then…"

His tight, muscled abs tensed and clenched. She nibbled and bit gingerly into his back, licking and kissing away the sting. He groaned loudly as his heavy breathing quickened again. She paused briefly, enjoying the sound of her handiwork. "You were on top of me," she began as she clawed her nails across his chest and down the front of him. "I was on top of you, then we were side by side and you were behind me and finally you were inside of me." She scratched down his back again.

"Now I have all kinds of fantasies of us together." Her hands traveled around his waist to the front of him again. She pressed her body close, molding to his back and feeling the waft of curls surrounding his manhood. It excited her boldness even more. She moved to stand in front of him. She looked down. He stood straight out—thick, long and hard as a black slate. She licked her lips, satisfied with her seduction. "Let's do it again."

"Cyanna," he groaned.

His guttural voice was lower and deeper than she'd ever heard before. It was husky and foreign. She knew she had excited him, but he was still holding back. She wanted all of his power inside of her. She smiled as she opened the robe and let it fall to the ground. She stood naked and watched as he stared down the length of her body. She turned around slowly, giving him a better view. Then she peeked over her shoulder at his expression. She could see he was close to exploding. She could almost feel the tremor of need surging though him.

She turned back and gripped him tight, pulling out the full length of his manhood. A deep throaty groan rolled through his chest. The solely masculine sound excited her. She moved closer, filling her hands with his hardened need and once more pulling playfully in long, slow strokes of pleasure. Then she rubbed her body against his, leaned in and licked his hardened nipples. She looked up to him. Their eyes connected, and the power she sought ruptured.

She stepped into the rain and began walking away backward. "You want me?" she taunted. The cool water poured all over her glistening body. "Come and get me," she tossed over her shoulder. Mikhail took one step forward and before he even realized it, he was standing right behind her.

She'd intended to continue walking but didn't take a step. Mikhail was there; she felt him and didn't move. "Cyanna, I can't stop," he groaned. "The curve of your neck." He leaned down and ravaged her neck while frantically wrapping his arms around her body. "The fullness of your breasts." He squeezed her breast, she moaned at his exquisite grip. "The depth of your body." He delved down between her legs, bending her forward.

She could feel his body trembling in need. Her legs weakened. She nearly passed out, but he held her tight.

"Don't stop," she muttered quickly.

"I couldn't stop even if I wanted to," he whispered ardently.

"Don't stop," she repeated.

"I can't stop loving you."

"Mikhail, I…" she began, but in the quick madness of a microsecond, Mikhail turned her around and pulled her into his arms. She gasped as his quick movement snatched her breath away. He held her tight, looking into her wanton eyes. She couldn't move. "Mikhail," she whispered again before his mouth fused with hers.

The kiss—a tangled, frenzied dance of twisting, turning tongues—was volatile. She wrapped her arms around his neck as he lifted her up. Her legs encircled his waist, and she felt the solid hardness of his erection press against her. He shifted her body, gripping her rear. While standing, in one quick powerful surge, he entered her. She tensed, throwing her head back. He leaned in, grabbing her breast and sucking hard. She dug her nails into his back and shoulders as her legs trembled wildly. This was what she wanted—the power and force of all of him. He surged into her, filling her over and over again. An instant later a bolt of rapture shot through her like blinding-white lightning. In her rapturous climax, she screamed his name. But he was nowhere near done with her.

She felt the steel of his strong muscles tighten, still holding her in place as he laid them down on the wet grass. Then her wild, relentless ride began again. He was fierce and feral in his pursuit of pleasure, and she met his abandoned intensity with equal fervor and zeal. He delved deeply into her; his pace quickened, sending her excitement raging as she anticipated the ultimate prize once more. Her breasts bounced in a joyous fury of climactic pursuit as he surged into her with relentless pleasure over and over and over again.

He brought her close, but just on the brink he slowed to a teasing, torturing pace, drawing each stroke in and out with deliberate languishing ease. She dug her nails into his shoulders as she held on, begging for the relief that only he could give her. He gave in, and in abandoned ecstasy she snatched her second orgasm of the night.

Then, just as she came, he thrust his hips into her one last time. He grabbed her rear in an iron-vice grip and exploded in a rage of intense pleasure. His body rocked and quaked in repeated climactic ripples.

Breathless and exhausted, he rolled over, and she immediately climbed on top of him. He was still hard enough for what she had in mind. He smiled at her as she slowly impaled herself. She sat straight up, letting the now-drizzling rain pour down the front of their glistening bodies. She rounded her hips to grind deeper as he cupped her breast and held her waist. Everything about this was methodical and sensual. She slowly rode him all the way to the brink of dawn.

Chapter 11

"Good morning."

Cyanna stirred and rolled over slowly. "Morning," she muttered sleepily as she opened her eyes. Mikhail walked over to the bed with two cups in his hands. He sat the cups down on the nightstand and then opened the drapes. Bright sunshine washed through the room instantly. Cyanna moaned.

"Rise and shine, sleepyhead."

"Uh, go away. It's Saturday. No one rises and shines on Saturday morning," she said as she pulled the sheet over her head.

"I have tea."

Cyanna peeked out from under the sheet and smiled at the cup in his hand. She dragged herself to sit up. He handed her a cup, and she took a timid sip. "Mmm, good tea," she said.

He sat down on the side of the bed and thoroughly examined her face. "Are you okay? How are you feeling?"

"I'm a little tired but, other than that, I'm fine."

"About what happened outside in the yard," he began. A myriad of memories from their early-morning love fest came to her. Mikhail had given her exactly what she'd asked for and she'd loved it. The last thing she remembered was lying on top of him, listening to his heartbeat. She presumed he had carried her up to bed. "You were different, and I was..." He paused.

"You were exhilarating, you were powerful and you were incredible," she finished for him.

"Actually, I was going to say overly aggressive."

"I liked it," she said with a mischievous glint in her eyes.

"You liked it?" he asked, surprised and curious.

She nodded and smiled as naughty thoughts slipped into her mind. "A lot. A little overly aggressive intensity now and then adds spice. So, don't hold back for me. I can take it. Okay?"

He smiled and nodded. "A little spice once in a while, okay."

"Good, so I guess you're not going to work today. Great idea, let's play hooky."

"Actually, I went. I'm back," he said, sipping his cup of tea.

She sat up in bed straighter. "You're back? What time is it?"

"It's still early," he said. "Are you hungry?"

"Actually I'm starved. What's for breakfast?"

"I thought we'd do something different."

"Like what?"

"We're going on a little trip."

"A trip where."

"To Cutter Island."

"Cutter Island, I never heard of it. Where is it?"

"It's a few miles off the coast."

"What's it like, crowded with vacationers?" she asked.

"No, not at all. It's a private island."

"Oh, a private island sounds interesting."

"It is. There's a large tree house in the center of the island with six master bedrooms, each with a private bath and balcony. The island has water, food, electricity and anything else you might possibly want and need."

"Hmm, so we can just go there and live forever."

He nodded. "Yes, we can, very easily."

"Sounds like I'm gonna like Cutter Island," she said, sipping her tea again. "Wait a minute. Is it a private island like the Midnight Madness Festival private island with clothing optional and hundreds of strangers there?"

He chuckled. "No, Cutter Island is very private and secluded. And for future reference, clothing is definitely optional when you and I are there alone together. But this trip we'll be there with other people."

"Other people like who?"

"The island is owned by my family. And, as a matter of fact, a few members of my family are already there for the weekend. They asked us to join them. I said we'd stop by."

She smiled brightly. Mikhail was taking her to meet

his family. "And exactly how are you going to introduce me to your family, as your baby mama?"

He laughed. "No, actually I thought I'd just use your name."

She smiled. "Okay, sounds like a plan. I'd love to go to Cutter Island with you. So, I guess I should get out of bed and get dressed." She tossed the sheet back. Mikhail gave her that look. She knew they wouldn't be leaving anytime soon.

An hour and a half later, Mikhail left to take care of a problem at the marina and run a few last-minute errands before they left. Cyanna stayed to pack and get ready for their overnight trip. Needing an overnight case, she found her smaller carry-on suitcase in one of the other bedrooms. She brought it back to the master bedroom, opened it and pulled out some clothes she'd put away since shopping. She also took out a small plastic bag she'd gotten from the pharmacy a month ago. She opened it and pulled out three at-home pregnancy tests. She read the package and directions on each. She decided she'd try one just in case.

She went into the bathroom, took the test and prepared to wait five minutes. Refusing to stay and stare at the plastic stick, she went back to the bedroom and began packing an overnight bag. She sorted through her clothes and pulled out a sarong and folded it up to take. Just as she grabbed for the matching bikini, her cell phone rang. Since few people called her, she picked up without looking at the caller ID.

"Hello," she said happily, expecting the caller to be Donna.

"Hello, Ms. Dupres?"

"Yes, who's this?" she asked, continuing to go through the clothes in the closet.

"Ms. Dupres, this is Gil Upton from Upton Investigations."

Cyanna immediately stopped packing. The signal was weak, and his voice kept going in and out.

"Yes, Mr. Upton, I can barely hear you. Can you speak up?"

"I'm sorry this is a bad connection. I'm on a flight into South America."

"What can I do for you?"

"You asked me to keep you informed of anything I might hear regarding your brother's body."

"Yes, I did. I had a memorial service, but I'd like to properly lay him to rest." She took a deep breath and slowly released it. "Have you found his body?"

"Actually, I believe I've found him."

Cyanna's stomach jumped and her head spun quickly as she staggered to sit down. "What, what do you mean you found him? Derek, he's dead."

"Ms. Dupres, I'm not sure, but I believe your brother, Derek Dupres, might still be alive."

"What?"

"I got a lead on another investigation I was following up on here in South America. A client's husband was kidnapped and held hostage for a time. It's possible the same thing might have befallen your brother."

"Hostage? I've never gotten a ransom note from anyone. Why didn't they contact me? Oh my God, all this time—it's been months."

"Ms. Dupres, I don't want you to get ahead of this. I still need to check this out thoroughly. I don't want to get your hopes up, but I needed to inform you of my findings."

"Yes, yes, I understand. So how did this happen?"

"As I said, I was investigating for another client when I came across a man I believe fits your brother's description."

"Then we need to get him out of there, now," she insisted.

"It may not be that simple. I retrieved my client's husband and our recon photos showed another man being held. I'd like to send you a photo. If—"

"Yes, yes, please send me the photo," she interrupted.

"If you can identify the man, then perhaps we can resolve your case, as well. I'll have to negotiate."

"Yes, yes, whatever the ransom is, I'll pay."

"It could get expensive."

Her cell beeped; she had a text message. "Mr. Upton, hold on, I think the picture just came." She opened the file and downloaded the picture. She covered her mouth, part from joy and part from shock. It was Derek. Tears flowed instantly. How could this be happening after all these months?

"Ms. Dupres, are you there?" Gil said.

"Mr. Upton, yes, yes, it's him. Please do whatever it is you need to do to get my brother home to me now. I don't care how much it costs—just do it," she demanded in no uncertain terms.

"I understand. I'll contact you as soon as my flight lands in Bogotá."

"Bogotá, Colombia. I'll meet you there."

"No, let me call you when I have more information," he said.

"Okay, and thank you, Mr. Upton." She disconnected the call while still staring at the photo of her brother. He looked thin and weak. Tears rolled down her face and fell onto her phone's screen. She put it down and went into the bathroom to grab a tissue, and she noticed the pregnancy test still sitting on the counter. She picked it up. Seeing the results, she sighed. Just then her cell phone rang again.

She ran back to it and answered anxiously, "Yes, hello."

"Cyanna."

"Donna."

"Hey, how's it going? Are you okay? You sound stressed."

"I don't know yet. Tell me, do you think Ammar's offer to perform in Qatar is still possible?"

"Are you actually considering it?" Donna asked.

"Yes, I need money fast, lots of money fast," Cyanna said.

"Are you kidding, of course it is. When I told him what you said after he doubled the offer, he doubled that offer. I was stunned. As a matter of fact, I was going to call and tell you so you can formally turn it down again. But can you believe it? That's quadruple the usual rate. The man is seriously jonesing."

"Actually, I might have to reconsider his offer."

"What do you mean? Why? I thought—"

"Mr. Upton called just now. He's the private investigator I hired when Derek went missing. He just sent me a picture of Derek in South America. He thinks he's been held hostage all this time."

"Say what?" Donna screeched.

"I don't know any details right now. But I know that if he's been a hostage all this time I'm going to need to get money together fast—a lot of money. I was hoping Ammar would give me the money in advance."

"Oh, you know he will. The man worships the ground you walk on. He'd give you anything you ask."

"Okay, great, please don't say anything to him right now. I'm going to need more details from Mr. Upton first."

"Yes, of course. I'll contact Ammar when you give me the word."

"Okay, thanks, Donna."

"Cyanna, I'm so happy Derek's alive."

"Me, too. I'll call you as soon as I hear something." She ended the call and opened the downloaded file again. Derek was alive. The words sank into her heart with ease. She smiled, laughed and then cried like baby. She picked up her plastic stick and looked at the two very pink lines. She grabbed the other two tests from the bag and took them. There was no mistake, two pink lines, two red lines and a plus sign; all three tests from three different manufacturers showed the same thing. She was pregnant.

She looked at her brother's picture again. She needed to take care of this now before she wouldn't be able to. She dug out her computer tablet and immediately searched for flights to Bogotá, Colombia. As soon as she found one, she made a reservation and continued with her travel plans. When she finished she sat back and closed her eyes.

This was the second time this morning her head spun like a spinning top. She opened her eyes. The dizzy feeling was still there. She staggered to the bathroom and splashed water on her face. The last thing she needed was to pass out on her way to Miami to get to Bogotá.

Mikhail got to the marina an hour later than he wanted, but staying with Cyanna just a few minutes more was always worth it. He slammed the car door and headed to the main office. As soon as he walked in, he saw Jumper and Fannie standing at the counter, drinking coffee and waiting. Jumper glanced at his watch much too obviously, and Fannie, as always, smiled brightly. "Good morning," she said in her usual joyful tone.

"Good morning. All set?" he inquired.

"Yep, since an hour ago," Jumper chastised.

"Unavoidable. Where's Cisco and Luther?" Mikhail asked as he headed to his office. Fannie and Jumper followed.

"Luther had an early-morning fishing excursion and Cisco got a call and said he'd be back in a few hours."

"Okay, let's do it," Mikhail said, sitting in his chair.

Fannie took her usual seat in front of the desk and Jumper leaned on the filing cabinet like he always did. This was their usual weekly planning meeting. Fannie began, running though and synchronizing the schedule on everyone's tablets and computers. They were fully booked up as usual. She had a few concerns regarding services, and he told them his idea about adding new services to their lineup. They agreed wholeheartedly.

The conversations continued. Mikhail listened and intently focused since he found his thoughts wandering from time to time. Of course they centered on Cyanna. As the meeting began to wrap up, the ultimate conclusion was that the next few months were going to be more than hectic. Mikhail knew his overworked crew wouldn't be able to handle the crushing rush and having a couple more hands on deck could only be an asset.

"Okay, I think it's time we step up our game. Fannie, I'd like you to look into getting Jumper another assistant, perhaps two. Luther's coming into his own as a full member of the crew, and if the last few years are any indication, we're gonna need the help. Also, I was thinking you could use some assistance in the office. Let's throw out some feelers for an office assistant for you, as well."

Fannie smiled and nodded. "Yes, I agree. I'll get started on this today."

"Good, are we done here?"

"Well, now that you mention it and since you're being generous," Luther began. "We need to talk about *Cyanna.*"

"What about her?" Mikhail asked quickly.

"She's brand-new and she's a beaut, but we need to tweak a few knobs and bobbles before we get her into the water." He gave a detailed description of everything he thought needed to be done before it was water-safe for clients. But since the boat was brand-new, Mikhail agreed to only a few of his upgrades.

"Okay, that's it. I'll be out at Cutter this afternoon and most of tomorrow." Luther nodded and Fannie itched to get started. "That's it."

Just as they headed out of the office, Cisco came in. "Hey," he said to Mikhail. "You got a minute?" The firm seriousness in his tone and eyes told Mikhail this had nothing to do with the marina.

"Let's go up to the crow's nest." Cisco followed Mikhail up to his private office. They closed the door. "Okay, what's up?"

"Please tell me the Cyanna from the other day is not Derek's sister." Mikhail didn't answer. "Man, are you nuts?"

"I know what I'm doing."

"You were just supposed to keep an eye on her, but sleep with her—"

"There's more to it," Mikhail said.

"What more could there be?" Cisco asked, shaking his head. Mikhail didn't answer. "See that's why I never take those babysitting assignments. They never turn out right. They always get complicated."

"I love her."

"Yeah, you can see that all over your face. So, what are you gonna tell her?"

"About what?" Mikhail asked.

"Dude, you knew all along that Derek was on assignment. She's not going to be happy."

"Let me worry about that. Just get me the extraction date."

Cisco shook his head and walked to the door. He paused a minute without turning around. "If it's any consolation, I envy you, man. Later."

Mikhail turned to look out the window. He knew he was not in an enviable position. When Cyanna found out what he was really doing, she was going to be furious. He shook his head.

He grabbed his stuff and headed out. He still needed to pick up a few things for Cutter Island, and, depending on how the next few days played out, this might be their last few days together.

Chapter 12

There was a car parked out front when Mikhail drove up to his home. He didn't recognize it, but he knew it was a rental. He turned off the ignition, reached over to grab the small bag sitting on the passenger seat and opened it. He pulled out the tiny velvet box he'd purchased in town before coming home and smiled, knowing this was the beginning of a new life for him. He slipped it into his pocket, got out, walked inside and headed upstairs to see her.

When he walked into their bedroom, Cyanna was packing her clothes.

"Hey, you don't need all that for Cutter. We're only going overnight," Mikhail said after he walked into the bedroom and saw Cyanna's clothes all over the bed and half-stuffed into her two suitcases.

She turned around. "Hey, I was gonna leave you a note."

His heart instantly sank. "Leave me a note saying what?"

"I have to go," she said. "Now, right now."

"What are you talking about? Where?"

"It's Derek—he's alive. I just found out."

Mikhail stared at her. It was like everything he feared just came true. "What do you mean he's alive? Who told you this?"

"Gil Upton, he's the private investigator from Miami. I hired him when the State Department wouldn't help me with answers. They told me that Derek was presumed dead, and I hired him to find his body."

"Gil Upton."

She nodded. "So, I need to go to him."

"No, you don't. This makes no sense," Mikhail said.

"But it does. This explains everything. I never could get any information from anybody at the State Department. I went there and sat for hours. I called. I sent emails and wrote letters. I even had Ammar ask around for me since his family is very influential. Nothing worked. All they said was that Derek was presumed dead. Then they said he was dead. But they were wrong—Derek is alive."

Mikhail could see the joy in her eyes. He hated to be the one to darken her glow, but it needed to be done. There was no way he could have her walking into the middle of a sensitive operation to save her brother, who certainly didn't need saving. "Where is he?" Mikhail asked.

"I don't know yet. Mr. Upton is going to call me with details. I have a picture." She grabbed her cell phone, found the picture and showed it to him.

Mikhail took the phone and looked at the photo. He shook his head slowly. "Cyanna, this isn't Derek."

"Yes, it is. I know what my brother looks like. That's him," she said, grabbing her cell to look at it again.

"No, it's not. You're just hoping it is because—"

"What is wrong with you?" she injected quickly. "Can't you see him? I thought you were Derek's friend." Her head took a major spin. She swayed, then slowly sat down on the bed. Mikhail hurried to quickly sit down beside her.

"Cyanna, what's wrong? Are you okay?" he asked.

She cupped her forehead in her hand and took a deep breath to gather herself. "I'm fine. I just don't get it. You're his friend."

"Yes, I am his friend," he said calmly, seeing how stressed and upset she was. "Cyanna, this is a tiny photo taken from a long distance on a cheap cell phone camera then enlarged to confuse you."

"Why are you saying that?" she asked tearfully as she stared at the photo of the man coming out of a small rustic building surrounded by verdant foliage and men with guns. She handed him the phone again.

"Look. See, that's Derek right there—he's alive. Mr. Upton was at the site to negotiate another hostage transfer and one of his associates took this picture. It's Derek, see? Mr. Upton is on a flight headed to Bogotá right now. There's no direct flight from here and all flights to Miami are booked up, so I'm driving to Miami. I already rented a car. I'm going to meet him there." She stood and continued packing her things.

"In Bogotá," he said, astonished, realizing this had gone way too far. She nodded busily. "No," Mikhail said.

She stopped and looked at him. "What?"

"I said no. There's no way I'm going to let you go to Colombia on a wild-goose chase to meet a man you barely know."

"I know him. I hired him," she insisted, zipping the case.

"Cyanna, listen to yourself. This makes no sense. Why would   "

"It makes perfect sense. What are you talking about?" she quickly interrupted him. "And if you are his friend, like you said you are, you'd understand why I need to go." She dropped the first suitcase on the floor and grabbed the other one.

He rushed over and took it from her. She released the handle. "I understand this man is conning you," he said.

"How can you say that? For the first time in months I actually have hope that my brother is still alive, and all you can say is I'm being conned." She shook her head furiously as tears began to flow again.

"That's not all I can say. I can say you're not going."

She shook her head. "I told you before, Mikhail, not to try to run my life." She grabbed the last few pieces of clothing, tossed them into the second suitcase, slammed it shut and zipped it. "I'm going."

"No, you're not," he said.

She laughed. "And how exactly are you going to hold me here—tie me to the bed?"

"That idea has merit," he snapped. She turned and glared at him. "Reason, I'll use reason to keep you here."

She shook her head. "Yeah, the only reason you want me to stay is because I'm pregnant with your child," she blurted out angrily, then stopped and looked at him. This wasn't how she'd planned to tell him. But she could see in his face it was already too late. His eyes darkened and a scowl deepened.

"You're what?" he said. "You're pregnant."

"I'm not sure yet. I haven't seen a doctor. I took tests."

"How many tests?" he asked.

She glanced over at the three test strips on the dresser. "Three home pregnancy tests—they were all positive results." He walked over and picked each one up and examined them carefully.

He turned, smiled and looked down at her stomach. "You're pregnant." He walked back over to her and swept her up in his arms. "You're pregnant," he repeated as he kissed her over and over again. "You're pregnant."

"Yes, maybe, it's possible."

"Well, we'll set up a doctor's appointment today and get—"

"No, Mikhail, nothing's changed. If anything I need to get to South America sooner. Every minute counts for me and for Derek."

"Are you seriously still thinking about going to Bogotá?"

"I have to. Derek—"

"Is fine," Mikhail said.

She stopped and glared at him suspiciously. "How do you know?"

He paused. "If indeed he is being held hostage, kidnappers don't hurt their payday. They're in it for the money," he said, covering quickly.

"Money," she said, remembering her conversation with Donna.

"What about it? Did Upton give you a number?"

"No, not yet. But I'm gonna need cash, I assume."

"I have money," he said.

"No, I'll get the money."

"How, from where, from whom?" he asked, looking at her. She knew she didn't need to answer his question because he already knew who she was going to get the money from. "Ammar," he gritted out.

"He's agreed to quadruple my fee for a single gig. I'm going to take his offer and ask for the money up front."

"No, you're not," he said determinedly.

"Seriously, what is it about me that makes you insist on trying to run my life? I'm going to Ammar, I'm taking his money and I'm going to Bogotá to get my brother."

Mikhail shook his head. "You have it all worked out."

"Yes, I do," she snapped.

"No, you don't," he snapped back.

She glared at him for a few minutes, then grabbed the handles on her rolling suitcases and moved to the door. He intercepted and stood in the way. "Mikhail, you need to move and let me go."

He dropped his head to her shoulder. "Cyanna, I can't. You don't understand. I can't."

"You don't understand. I don't have a choice. He's my big brother. There's nothing he wouldn't do for me. He saved me. He saved my life at the risk of his own. I have to do this."

Mikhail shook his head. "No, you don't. Derek would never forgive me if I let you go."

Her heart stammered and trembled. "You knew. All this time. You let me suffer thinking my brother was dead and you knew he was alive. What are you, some kind of sadist? You get off messing with people's minds?"

"No, Cyanna, listen to me—"

"No, I've heard enough. You knew Derek was alive and you did nothing to help him."

"I couldn't."

"So what now? He just rots in some dirty, filthy jail in South America and I'm just supposed to do nothing. And what about me—all this time you knew, saw me in pain and said nothing. What was I?" she asked pointedly. Then she knew the answer. "I was a job? All this between us was just an assignment to keep me quiet and out of the way while you boys played your games, right?"

"I can't," he repeated softly.

"You don't have to say anything. I know I'm right. I know a betrayal when I see one."

"Cyanna—" he said.

"Don't."

"I love you, Cyanna," he said. She gasped quietly as

his words sunk into her heart. "I never thought I would ever find a woman like you, but I have. I love you with all my heart and soul. But I can't let you go to Bogotá or anywhere else." Cyanna's body swayed as her head spun wildly again. Mikhail held her arms to still her. "Cyanna—"

"Mikhail, you can't stop me." After a few minutes he stepped out of her way, but he took the suitcase handles from her. She looked up into his eyes. She knew he wasn't going to change his mind. He rolled the cases back across the room to the closet.

She continued walking to the door. "Fine, I'll just buy clothes when I get there."

"What was it going to say?" he asked.

She stopped. "What was what going to say?" she asked.

"The note you were going to write me," he said. "Were you even going to tell me about the baby?" She remained silent. "You weren't, were you?"

Her heart sank that he would think that. "Yes, of course I was going to tell you—when I got back."

He picked up the pregnancy test strips again and stared at them. "You're not going."

She secured her purse and the small overnight bag on her shoulder and hurried downstairs. Unfortunately the quick movements nearly had the stairs coming up to meet her. She staggered but kept her balance enough to reach the first floor.

She hurried out and went straight to the rental car. She got in just as Mikhail followed her outside. He called to her. She started the engine and drove off quickly. She was headed down the driveway, watching him in her rearview mirror. She saw him run to his car. She pressed the accelerator down and redirected her attention to the front windshield. A second later everything went black.

Chapter 13

What seemed like a million lifetimes in slow motion to Mikhail was merely a few seconds in reality. He watched the car continue straight as the driveway curved to the left. The majestic row of mahogany trees stood as the car's sole deterrent. Without even realizing it, he exited his car and started to run to her as he called out her name. The car ran straight into a tree. The impact was instant, and the loud whining crackle of crumpled steel resounded in his ears. The tree shook. A branch several feet up tumbled down onto the windshield. The sickening sound of glass shattering stopped him. His heart fell. He looked up. Another branch, much thicker, swayed and hovered precariously above, threatening to fall. "Cyanna," he whispered, then ran.

He got to the driver's side door and grabbed the handle. He yanked it hard, nearly lurching his shoulder out of the socket. It was locked from the inside. He could see that Cyanna was thankfully belted, but she was unconscious. There was blood on her forehead and on her hand. He called out to her repeatedly. She was breathing, but she didn't move. Shattered, broken glass was everywhere.

He tried all the doors as he called 911 and gave them his information. When they were on the way, he ran back to his car and got his window-breaking tool. He ran back to the rental car and smashed the passenger rear door window and unlocked the front seat door. Within seconds he was inside the car, sitting beside her. She was slumped forward and to the side. "Cyanna, sweetheart, can you hear me?" She didn't answer.

He reached down and unlatched her seat belt, then unlocked her door. He got back out, rushed around and opened her door. He eased her out of the car and carried her several yards away from the accident scene. He heard the faint sound of sirens coming closer. Then a sheriff's car with lights flashing came barreling into his driveway. It barely stopped before his cousin Stephen got out and ran to his side. He was vehemently yelling at dispatch to send additional help.

"Mikhail, what happened?" he asked as the sirens grew louder.

Breathless, Mikhail looked at his cousin. "She missed the curve. The car went into the tree."

"Are you hurt? Were you in the car?" Stephen asked. Mikhail didn't answer. "Mikhail, listen to me. Are you hurt?"

Mikhail looked up at Stephen and shook his head. "No."

"Were you in the car?"

"No."

"Okay, hold on, help is here," he said as he stepped away to direct the fire truck and ambulance speeding toward them. An EMT got out with her bag and ran to Mikhail and Cyanna. Her partner hurried to the back of the ambulance and pulled out a stretcher and rolled it over. A fire truck arrived.

"Okay, Mikhail, hold back and let the EMTs take care of her."

"No, I got her."

Stephen grabbed his cousin's arm. "Listen to me. I know what she means to you. Trust us—we got this. Now let her go."

Mikhail released her slowly as Stephen gently eased her unconscious body down to the ground. Two EMTs and a fireman immediately surrounded her. Mikhail stepped away with Stephen at his side. "Stephen, she's pregnant," he said.

Stephen looked at Mikhail, then at Cyanna and then back at Mikhail. The unmistakable look of fear and unconditional love in his eyes was heart wrenching. "Okay," he said softly. "Okay."

Just then the hovering branch fell, slicing the front windshield in half, taking out the steering wheel and landing on the passenger seat. Everyone stopped and looked and then went back to what they were doing. A second later another car came to a sudden stop nearby.

Dominik got out with his bag and ran over. "Are you hurt?" he called out to Mikhail.

"No. Dom, help her. She's pregnant."

Dominik looked at Mikhail and then at Stephen. Stephen nodded and motioned to Cyanna. Dominik ran to her as the EMTs parted for him. Shauna got out of the car and hurried to Stephen and Mikhail. "What can I do?" she asked anxiously.

"Where are your keys?" Stephen asked Mikhail.

He shook his head. "I think I dropped them by my car."

Shauna looked at his car still parked in front of the house. She nodded, knowing exactly what to do. "I'll lock up the house and take care of everything here." She turned and ran across the lawn to the house.

Stephen and another officer walked Mikhail farther away from the scene. Mikhail gave them Cyanna's name and other pertinent information. Stephen purposely maneuvered his cousin in the opposite direction as the EMTs put Cyanna on the stretcher. "Mikhail, let's get in my car. I'll take you to the hospital."

Mikhail shook his head. "No, I have to stay with her." He turned around as the stretcher rounded the ambulance. Dominik was at Cyanna's side.

"She's leaving now. Let's go." They hurried to Stephen's car as the EMTs got into the ambulance.

Stephen followed with his lights and siren on. Neither spoke as Stephen concentrated on driving and Mikhail focused on getting to Cyanna. They arrived at the hospital just as the ambulance pulled up. An emergency medical team was standing in the ambulance bay waiting. As soon as the ambulance stopped, they ascended.

Mikhail and Stephen got out of the car and stood watching as Dominik and his E.R. team rolled Cyanna inside. Mikhail went to follow, but Stephen grabbed his arm. Mikhail looked at him threateningly. Stephen shook his head and gripped his arm tighter. "Mikhail, there's nothing you can do right now. You know Dom is an exceptional doctor. Leave this to him and his team. Give them a few minutes to assess Cyanna's condition."

Mikhail jerked his arm away and moved to follow them inside. "Cuz, I'll have to beat you down, crack your head and break your legs if you go in there—and not necessarily in that order. Now I know you don't want that, do you?"

Mikhail stopped. His body jerked as his shoulders trembled. He shook his head and turned to his cousin. The hoped-for laughter in Mikhail's eyes made Stephen smile. They chuckled, then laughed. Stephen knew that the biting tension and stress of the past few minutes needed an escape. He also hoped he wouldn't have to follow through with his threat.

Mikhail nodded. "Okay." They walked off to the side. "I can't lose her, Stephen." He looked over at the closed bay doors.

"I know. You won't."

"I love her so much. I never thought…"

"I know."

"And she drives me crazy, still I can barely breathe without her. I think about her every second of every day. She's a part of me that I never knew I was missing. She's in my heart, in my soul, in every breath I take. I love her."

"Yep, that's what they do to us. Thank God, huh?"

Mikhail nodded. "Yeah, thank God."

"Hey, congratulations, Dad," Stephen added.

Mikhail smiled and nodded. "She hasn't seen a doctor yet. But she took three at-home tests and they were all positive."

"Like I said, congratulations, Dad," Stephen said, then bumped Mikhail's fist and patted his shoulder. Mikhail winced. Stephen looked at his hand and saw blood. He looked at Mikhail's back, seeing a dark wetness on the shoulder and sleeve of his shirt. A thin crimson line trickled down. "You're bleeding—let's go."

Mikhail looked down at his arm. He didn't feel a thing or realize he'd been cut.

They went inside and one of the E.R. nurses met them. Mikhail and Stephen went with her. An anxious, apprehensive hour later, Mikhail and Stephen sat in Dominik's office. The door opened. They turned. Shauna walked in. "Hey," she said. "Any news?"

"No," Mikhail grumbled.

"Soon, I'm sure Dominik is being very thorough."

"How'd you get to the house so fast?" Stephen asked Shauna.

"We were on our way home then Dominik got a call from the E.R. after the ambulance went out. They told him there had been an accident at Mikhail's, so we went straight there."

"Thanks for taking care of the house, Shauna."

She hugged him warmly. "That's what sisters do,"

she said, knowing she had never been able to say that before. And now being married to Dominik and a member of the Coles family was her heart's dream come true. "I heard you needed attention."

"Yeah, I guess I cut my shoulder after I broke the window and tried to get the door unlocked. I didn't even know it."

"Adrenaline," she surmised. "Are you okay?"

He nodded. "Yeah, fine, except for waiting for your husband to get in here and tell me something."

"Like I said, he's very thorough."

There was a knock on the door. Shauna, nearest, opened it.

Natalia, David, Tatiana and Spencer came in. The growing gathering of family hugged and kissed each other, happy to be together. "Hey, what happened to you?" Tatiana asked, seeing Mikhail in a hospital scrub shirt.

"I cut my shoulder. I'm fine."

"How's Cyanna?" Natalia asked.

"We don't know yet," Mikhail said.

"Wait, I just called you less than an hour ago, I thought you were on Cutter," Stephen said.

"We were," David said.

"Yeah, but you got here so fast—that's impossible."

"Obviously you've never been in a speed boat with Spencer Cage behind the wheel," David said.

"That's right. My hubby can seriously cut through water," Tatiana said proudly.

"Fast, like at warp speed," Natalia chimed in. "Impressive."

"Ah, come on. We weren't going that fast," Spencer said.

David chuckled. "I know daredevil stuntmen who could take a few lessons from this guy. Nice driving, my man," David said as he and Spencer shook hands.

"All right, all right, maybe we were going a little swift," Spencer confessed.

"Looks like I'm gonna have to give some waterway speeding tickets out," Stephen joked. They all laughed, knowing they didn't exist.

The door opened. Dominik walked in and looked around. His not-so-small office was packed with family. "Hey, what are you all…"

Everyone parted to let Mikhail step forward. Dominik went to his brother, smiling. "She's fine. She has a few abrasions and some cuts, also a slightly sprained wrist and bruises, but she's gonna be just fine. Her blood pressure is high, so we're going to keep her for a few days for observation."

"Is she awake?"

"Yes."

"In a lot of pain?" he asked.

"No, nothing extreme. Of course, I'd rather not prescribe any type of strong pain medication."

"Can I see her?" Mikhail asked anxiously.

"Give the staff a few minutes to get her into her room. They're gonna call me when she's settled. Also, I gave her a little something to help her relax and sleep. It's very safe for her in her condition. And speaking of which, I did the official test and I'm delighted to be able to confirm." Dominik shook Mikhail's hand. "Congratulations." Mikhail beamed.

"Wait, congratulations for what?" Tatiana asked.

Mikhail turned to his family. "Cyanna's pregnant."

The room erupted in a joyous impromptu celebration, then just as quickly they all quieted down, realizing where they were. Hugs, kisses, handshakes and cheerful laughter still resounded. "Okay, okay, everybody out," Dominik said. "We can take this celebration over to the house. By the way Mom and Dad called. They're on the way."

"Why don't you all come over to our house?" Stephen said. "Mia's there with the baby and Brice and Jayden."

Dominik and Mikhail stayed behind, promising to catch up later. "Stephen," Mikhail called out before he left. Stephen turned and hung back. Mikhail walked over to him. "Thanks for everything." They shook hands and hugged.

"It's all about family," Stephen said. "I'm just glad I didn't have to beat you down." He and Mikhail laughed. Then Stephen left.

"Beat you down?" Dominik repeated.

"It's a long story."

"I heard you needed a dressing."

"Yeah," Mikhail said. "It's all good."

"Okay, let me know if you have any problems."

"Dom, she's gonna be okay, right?" Mikhail asked.

Dominik smiled and nodded. "Yes, as a professional medical doctor and E.R. department head, Cyanna Dupres is going to be fine as long as she takes care of herself and the baby."

"So what caused the crash?" Mikhail asked.

"She told me she'd been dizzy all day and nearly fainted a few times. She thinks she passed out behind the wheel."

"Passed out," Mikhail repeated.

Dominik nodded. "Yes, her blood pressure is high. We're working to get it down now."

"How serious is that?"

"I'm not going to lie to you, Mikhail. It can be very serious. Starting a pregnancy like this isn't good. Cyanna has a mild case so far, but unchecked this can be very dangerous to both mother and fetus, particularly in early pregnancy. But right now the good thing is she's in excellent health with no preexisting conditions.

"She'll be back to the house in a few days and she's going to have to stay calm and completely stress-free. You need to make sure she stays that way."

"I understand."

"Good. So, ideally, I'd like her on bed rest for the next few weeks, but I'll be happy with her staying in the house and staying calm. The last thing we want or need are complications."

"Complications," Mikhail repeated and sighed heavily.

"You want to tell me about it?" Dominik said.

"Cyanna and I have an arrangement. We both wanted a child, so we agreed to have one together. That's why she's been staying at the house. But now that she's pregnant, she's leaving me."

"What do you mean leaving you?"

"It was all part of the agreement we made. We weren't supposed to get emotionally involved. But I can't let her go."

"You're in love with her," Dominik stated.

"Does it show that much?"

"Yeah, pretty much."

"Does everybody know?"

"I think maybe there are a few centuries-old mummies in the local museum who don't know yet, but other than that…"

Mikhail smiled. "Yes, I love her. Four months ago I was sent to her because she was beginning to endanger her brother's job. When she opened the door, my heart jumped a beat. It's been like that since then." Dominik nodded. "I thought if I walked away that would be enough, but I kept thinking about her. And then she showed up with a proposal I couldn't refuse. She wanted a baby, our baby."

"And you agreed."

"Yes, I agreed. I guess I hoped that maybe she'd feel—"

"She called out for you as soon as she regained consciousness. I have a feeling she loves you, too. Have you told her you love her? I'm sure she won't leave if she knows how you feel about her."

"I did. I told her. She was leaving me when she had the accident. Now, as soon as she gets better she's gone."

"She lives in New York. Move there."

"It's not that simple. Her brother is a friend, a co-worker," he specified pointedly.

Dominik nodded. "Okay." He immediately understood.

"He's unavailable, and she wants to go find him in Bogotá."

"Bogotá, Colombia?" Dominik clarified. Mikhail nodded. "No, no, that's out of the question. With her high blood pressure, a trip like that could jeopardize her and the pregnancy. She can't go. Do whatever you need to do."

"I intend to," Mikhail assured him.

Dominik's phone rang. He answered, nodded and agreed a couple of times, then ended the call and turned to Mikhail. "Come on, I'll walk you up to the room. She's gonna be a little groggy."

Mikhail nodded silently as they headed out of the office and down the hall to the stairs. They walked up to the second floor in silence. When they got to the room, Dominik paused. "Okay, I'm gonna pop in for a few minutes first. I'll be back to get you."

Mikhail agreed and leaned against the wall outside Cyanna's room. He thought about what his brother had said: stress-free.

"Mikhail, she's half-asleep," Dominik said.

He walked in. The lights in the room were dimmed. Cyanna was lying in the hospital bed with monitors all around her. Her left hand and wrist was bandaged and she had a dressing on the side of her forehead.

"Are you sure she'll be—" Mikhail began.

"Yes, she'll be fine in a few days."

Cyanna opened her eyes slowly and looked at the two Coles brothers. Concern and worry scarred Mikhail's face. "Hey, guys." She smiled and held her hand out to Mikhail. He hurried to her side.

Dominik followed. "Are you in any pain right now?" he asked Cyanna.

"Just a little, but I think I'll live," she said.

He smiled at her humor. "You will. If the pain gets worse tonight, let the nurse on duty know. I wrote a pain medication prescription in your chart if needed."

"Okay, thank you."

"No problem, just no more scares. You had the whole family worried." She nodded and jokingly crossed her heart and held up three fingers. "Good, I'll let you two talk, but not too long. You need your rest." She nodded. Dominik turned to Mikhail. "I'm out. Call me if you need me. Good night."

"I will. Thanks, Dom. Good night."

Mikhail leaned down and kissed Cyanna tenderly on the lips. "How are you?" he whispered.

"I have a sledgehammer headache and my chest feels like an anvil is sitting on it, but I'm sure I look worse than I feel," she said slowly. She held up her bandaged wrist and looked at it, then dropped it heavily back to her side and winced.

"You look beautiful, as usual."

"Liar," she joked.

"I would never lie to you," he said earnestly.

"So, I hear it's official. You're gonna be a father," she said, smiling. It was obvious the medication to help her sleep was working.

"Yeah, we did it." She placed their hands on her

stomach. They smiled, quietly pleased. "Mikhail, about what happened today—"

"We'll talk about it later. Right now you need to rest and not get stressed out. That's an order."

"Still trying to run my life," she said, yawning.

"Yes, this time I definitely am," he confessed.

She shook her head. "Remind me to be mad at you later."

He smiled and nodded. "Yeah, okay. I'll remind you." He picked up her hand and kissed it.

"What time is it?" she asked.

"Late."

"I need to get out of here," she said sleepily.

"No. You need to stay exactly where you are and get well. I'll take care of everything else."

"You can't."

"Yes, I can and I will."

She nodded slowly and smiled happily. "You said you loved me."

"Yes, I did. I do love you."

"Good, because I love you, too," she muttered softly.

"I think it's time we should talk about the third condition to our deal," he said.

She opened her hooded eyes and chuckled. "You have lousy timing. You wait until I ram a car into a tree, explode an air bag in my face and can barely focus on speaking to talk about the third condition?"

"Yeah, that's right."

She grinned. "Okay, what is it?"

"Will you marry me?"

She didn't speak. A single tear slid down her cheek as

she reached up to touch the side of his face. She softly closed her eyes.

"We'll talk later—get some rest." He stood and walked over to the door to leave.

"Mikhail," she called quietly. He turned quickly and came back to the side of the bed. "Will you stay with me until I fall asleep?"

"Yes, of course I will," he said, softly kissing her cheek.

"Thank you." She closed her eyes again and took a deep breath, smiling. A few minutes later she slept.

Mikhail stayed another few hours. He sat by her bedside the whole time just in case she woke up again. Fitful at first, now her stillness and even breathing showed she was resting peacefully.

He stood, leaned over and kissed her lips tenderly. He smiled and kissed her stomach. "I'll be back as soon as I can," he whispered. He reached into his pocket and pulled out a stunning black diamond ring. He carefully adjusted and pulled back the bandage on her hand and wrist and placed the ring on her finger. "You probably won't remember any of this and that's okay. As long as you know I love you."

When Mikhail left that night, he didn't go home; instead he headed to the marina. He left Cisco a message telling him he needed some equipment. He went to his office and began doing what he did best, reconnaissance. In his former occupation he'd been an intel specialist. His job was to go in, acquire live usable intel and then exit. He had numerous unnamed sources and informants on just about every level. If there was information, he got it. Two hours later he learned what he needed. There was a planned insertion into Central America with an extraction team on board. He had all intentions of joining that operation.

He made a few calls and finally got the answer he wanted. The plan included transportation, satellite pin-point intel and enough munitions just in case they ran into trouble. He gathered his gear to move out. Just before dawn he headed to the dock with his bags to load his boat and get to the designated location. It wasn't surprising that Cisco showed up dressed and ready. "Hey, I thought you might be going fishing, so I figured I'd tag along. You haven't done this in a while."

"I still have my skills and I'm gonna need you to keep an eye on the shop," Mikhail said, "I might be a while."

"It's my day off," Cisco said, dropping one of his bags. "And I feel like going fishing."

Mikhail knew trying to talk Cisco out of something was futile. He nodded. Cisco tossed his other bag up. Mikhail caught it and dropped it on deck next to his.

"You have a way in?" Cisco asked.

"Yeah, I made a few calls. There's an active mission out of Miami, headed to Panama in thirty-six hours. I'm gonna shadow their mission, then do a cargo drop. I have a jump seat lined up. I'm sure I can get one more."

"And getting to the site?" Cisco asked.

"I have a friend in the camp. He'll hook us up."

"Sounds good, but there might be a small problem with the first part of the plan. The thing is word got out that you were going fishing and a couple of old buddies wanted to come with."

"What couple of old buddies?" Mikhail asked.

Cisco grinned at the headlights turning into the parking lot. "Looks like you have company."

Mikhail glanced at his watch. It was a few minutes after five in the morning and way too early for Jumper, Luther, Fannie or any boating clients to be coming in. The vehicle's headlights turned off before it stopped. Three men got out and began walking down the dock toward them.

"Harper, Stone and Dyson," Cisco said.

"I wonder how they found out I was going fishing."

"I might have mentioned it to them in passing. So, you're gonna have to nix the jump seats. Harper arranged for a UH-60 Black Hawk pickup off the coast of Cutter Island in two hours. They're gonna take us directly to the camp. Stone has some new satellite recon gadgets he wants to try out. He's got a fixed location on positioning."

"Sounds like you have it all worked out," Mikhail said. Cisco nodded. "And what about Dyson—what's he bringing to the table?"

Cisco shrugged and chuckled. "Dyson was just bored at home and wanted a little action."

Mikhail shook his head as his friends walked down the dock to the boat. "Well, I guess we'll see what we can do about that." A half hour later they were cutting through waves headed west to Cutter Island.

Chapter 14

Midmorning the next day, Cyanna opened her eyes and looked around. The thick haze in her head slowly began to clear, leaving a pounding headache in its place. She was in a hospital room; that much was clear. But she had no idea how she'd gotten there. The curtains were drawn. Through a haze, her memory started to clear—the car, the tree and "Mikhail," she whispered.

She focused harder, cutting through the fog. She remembered people talking about a car accident. What she did know for sure was that her head was pounding and every muscle in her body ached. She reached up and touched her forehead, then saw the bandage on her hand and wrist. A spike of pain shot through her as she lowered her arm gently back to the raised pillow. Her wrist hurt, and her fingers were numb. She took a deep breath and then released it slowly. The pain subsided.

She remembered the argument she'd had with Mikhail. Then she remembered Colombia. He didn't want her to go to Bogotá to help her brother. Derek was alive. She ran out of the house and got in the car and that's when everything seemed to get blurry. She fainted. But there was more. She looked up at the large bouquets of flowers sitting on shelf behind the two chairs. One had a yellow satin ribbon that read, "Congratulations."

A few seconds later there was a knock on the door. "Yes, I'm awake. Come in," she said.

The door opened. A woman stuck her head in the room smiling. "Good morning," she said softly. "I don't know if you remember me. My name is Shauna Coles. Dominik, Mikhail's brother, is my husband."

Cyanna smiled. "Yes, of course I remember you. We met when Mia and Stephen had their baby about a month ago. Good morning."

Shauna, carrying a large shopping bag, came all the way into the room and stood by the bed. "How are you feeling?" she asked, glancing at the monitors.

"I'm a little sore. But I guess that's to be expected."

Shauna nodded. "I'm sure the soreness will be gone soon. Oh, I brought something—your purse from the car. I thought you might want some of your own things and of course your cell phone. I'd be completely lost if I went all morning without my cell. I hope you don't mind, it was beeping, so I charged it for you."

"No, not at all, thank you so much," Cyanna said.

Shauna placed the cell phone on the serving tray

angled across the bed, then turned and put her purse in the closet.

Cyanna quickly glanced at her phone messages. There was a missed call and two messages from Donna but nothing from Gil Upton.

Shauna turned and noted the slight frown on Cyanna's face. "I hope there was no bad news."

"No, I was just expecting a call with some information. I haven't gotten it yet. I really appreciate you bringing my purse."

"No problem, it's my pleasure," Shauna said, admiring the flowers.

"No, really, it was very thoughtful of you."

"Well, of course. You're part of the family.

"Actually, I'm not really part of the family. My baby is."

"Believe me, Cyanna, you are, as well."

"I don't know, maybe one day," Cyanna said wishfully. "Maybe."

"Cyanna, listen to me. I've been a loner all my life. I was an only child and all of a sudden I was an orphan. I wasn't used to family and closeness, but as soon as I met and married Dominik I became part of the most loving family I could ever imagine. There's a siblinghood that's like nothing you'll ever feel. The Coles family is extremely close. When one is hurting, we all feel it. You're part of this family now."

They continued talking about the Coles and who was married to whom and who had children. Then they talked about their lives and were surprised at how much they had in common. Shauna told her about her job in the hospital, and Cyanna told Shauna about her life on the road performing. An hour passed quickly.

There was another knock on the door. "Come in," Cyanna said.

Dominik walked in and smiled happily at his wife. "Hello, ladies," he said, then walked over to Shauna. He kissed her lovingly.

She returned his loving gesture, smiling. "We were just talking about you, well, more specifically, the Coles family siblings."

Dominik chuckled. "I hope it was good things."

"Yes, all good things," Shauna assured him, smiling at Cyanna. "Well, now that your doctor is here, I'm gonna get back to work." She turned to Cyanna. "Call me if you need anything or get lonely up here. We'll talk later."

Cyanna smiled. "I will, and thanks for everything."

Shauna winked at her new husband. "Stop by when you get a chance, Doc," she said to him, then walked out.

"She's a wonderful woman," Cyanna said.

Dominik nodded as he washed and dried his hands. "Yes, she is. She's the love of my life," he said. He tossed the paper towel into the trash can and walked over to the hospital bed. "So, how are you feeling today?"

"My memory is clearing, but my wrist hurts like crazy. I can barely hold my hand up without throbbing pain."

"Understandably, although the accident was relatively minor, the injuries you sustained are common due to air bag deployment. You have bruises, a few abrasions, and you have a sprained wrist, which will—"

"Wait, a sprain?" she said anxiously as her heart jumped and her stomach clenched. "But I play a violin for a living. How am I going to perform if I can't even hold an instrument?"

"Cyanna, you need to calm down."

"Calm down, are you kidding me? Do you have any idea how many classical musicians have had their careers ended by a simple sprain?" She held up her hand to show him, then winced in pain. "Oh my God, how am I ever going to perform? I can't. My career is over. I'll never be able to—"

"All right, all right, calm down. Your hormones and your adrenaline is running high right now. There's no need to get upset. You'll be back to playing the violin in a few weeks without any loss of function as long as you take care of it now. We'll do our part. You'll need to do yours."

"Yes, I will. Okay."

"Now, as I was saying, you have very minor tear damage to the ligament."

"I guess that would explain the pain," she said.

"Yes," he said as he carefully lifted her wrapped hand to examine the wrist. She winced as he slowly pulled the gauze wrappings down. He saw the ring that Mikhail told him that he had put on her finger. "It looks good. Leave the bandage on and keep your arm elevated—we'll do the rest. Any other pains?" he asked.

Cyanna also told him about her persistent throbbing headache. He explained that the accident and her high blood pressure were more than likely the culprits and that she should be feeling better in a few days. He talked to her about the baby's health and the high blood pressure's effect on both her and the fetus. He also reminded her of the best ways to combat her high blood pressure. Since she was physically healthy, exercised regularly, didn't drink or smoke, ate well and basically took care of herself, she needed to reduce all stress levels and added anxiety in her life.

She nodded her understanding. "So, when can I get out of here?" she asked.

"Don't tell me you're ready to leave us already," he joked.

"I just have things to do, important things that need my attention," she said.

"I'm sure there's nothing so important that it can't wait a few days."

"It can't," she said earnestly.

"Cyanna, I'm not sure you understand what I'm saying to you."

"Doctor, Dominik, I understand what you're saying but—"

"Cyanna, there is no but, and no exceptions. I'm not only talking to you as a medical professional. I'm also speaking as a soon-to-be uncle. Whatever you think you need to do that adds stress to your life right now, don't do it. The weight of the world does not rest on your shoulders alone. Trust me on this. Let it go. Let others take care of it, at least for right now."

She sighed heavily, nodding. There was no way she'd jeopardize her child. "I understand."

"Good, now get some rest. I'll stop back later."

As soon as Dominik left, Cyanna called Donna.

"Hey, I tried calling you and left a couple of messages. I didn't get an answer, so I assumed you were traveling. Are you in South America?"

"No, actually I'm in the hospital."

"You're what?"

"I'm fine, I'm fine. I had a little car accident."

"Where, when, how?"

"Great questions. I think I fainted behind the wheel while driving and I crashed a rental car into a tree."

"Oh my God, Cyanna, you could have been killed. Okay, how injured are you? What are the doctors saying?"

"Like I said, I'm fine, but they found I have high blood pressure and I sprained my wrist when the air bag went off."

"Oh no, a sprained wrist," Donna said softly.

"It's just pulled ligaments. And it's my left hand, not my bow hand. The doctor said I should be as good as new in a few days and even better in a few weeks. He actually said I'd be without any loss of function as long as I take care of it now."

"Well, by all means listen to the doctor and do exactly what he says."

"He also said it would be unwise to go to Bogotá."

"Yes, I definitely agree. To tell you the truth, I didn't like the idea of you going to South America alone anyway. It sounded way too dangerous. What else did the doctor say?" Donna asked.

"He confirmed that I'm pregnant."

"Oh, Cyanna, that's wonderful," she nearly shrieked with joy in the cell phone's receiver. "This is fantastic news. I'm gonna be an aunt. I can't wait. I'm so happy for you and Mikhail, and I can't wait to spoil my new niece or nephew."

Cyanna smiled happily. "I'm so happy, you can't even imagine."

"I know Mikhail must be thrilled, as well. And I know he'll make sure you listen to the doctor."

"The doctor just happens to be his brother," Cyanna said.

"Even better, there's nothing like a doctor in the family."

There was a knock on the door and a nurse peeked in and smiled. "Donna, I have to go. I'll call you later."

The rest of the day was relatively quiet. She rested and listened to music and watched mindless TV. At one point she nodded off and dreamed Mikhail was there with her. He was standing beside her bed, holding her hand. He told her that everything would be okay and that she needed to take care of herself and the baby. But when she woke up he wasn't there.

The dream wasn't real, but this was. She rubbed her stomach gently and smiled. This was why she had come to Key West. She finally had exactly what she wanted, a child. She lay in bed, thinking about when she could have conceived. She hoped it was the night on the boat beneath the stars. There was something about that night that had changed her. Now it wasn't so much about having a baby as it was about having a family.

Mikhail would always be part of her family even

if she wasn't part of his. She remembered waking up in the middle of the night and seeing Mikhail standing over her bed. They had talked, but she had no idea what about. Then, in the blink of an eye, he was gone. She hadn't seen him since. By midnight she realized he wasn't coming to see her.

The next two days were much different. From midmornings until late in the evenings her hospital room was a revolving door. She'd been visited by most of the Coles, including Mikhail's parents. They came down from Marathon just to meet and see her. She met Nikita and Chase Buchanan, just back from their extended honeymoon in Alaska. And of course having mega movie star David Montgomery and his wife, Natalia, plus music mogul Spencer Cage with his wife, Tatiana, standing around her bedside was totally unreal. Everyone was friendly and accepting. She just wished Mikhail was there with her.

Chapter 15

Cyanna was feeling much better. She'd been in the hospital for four days, and she was ready to go home. She talked to a nutritionist, a gynecologist and a stress management specialist. Her wrist didn't hurt as much, and her headache was completely gone. She was still stiff and bruised, but she was also delightedly pregnant.

It had been days since Cyanna had seen Mikhail. He'd been there with her the first night, of that she was certain. After that he wasn't. Whenever she asked someone in the family about him, the story was always the same thing—he'll be in as soon as he can. But he never came. She was told to focus on getting better and she did. Her blood pressure was down and today she was leaving the hospital.

She got up early, showered and changed into her street clothes. She sat on the side of the bed, waiting for Dominik to arrive and discharge her. Surprisingly he hadn't been in since early morning the day before. Another doctor came in to see her in the evening and Shauna stopped by before she went home. But as long as someone signed her discharge papers she'd be happy.

Her cell phone rang. She picked it up and checked the caller ID. She recognized Donna's phone number and answered. "Hey, girl," Cyanna said joyfully. "What's up? How are you?"

"I should be asking you that question. How are you feeling today?" Donna asked.

"Much better," she said happily.

"Sorry, kiddo, but you don't sound much better."

"Trust me. I sound and look a lot better than I was a few days ago."

"So when are you getting out of there?"

"My new doctor said I'll be discharged later this afternoon, but I haven't seen Dominik yet. I saw him yesterday morning and that's it. Another doctor came in last night and again earlier this morning. I asked about Dominik, and she said he was out of the hospital on personal business."

"Okay, when are you getting the bandage off your wrist?"

"In a few days," Cyanna said.

"Good. You need to start practicing again. Have you decided if you're coming back to New York right away or staying there?"

Cyanna thought a moment, then shook her head. "I don't know yet. I'll probably go back to New York in a few days."

"Are you sure?"

Cyanna sighed heavily. "To tell you the truth, I don't know."

"Cyanna, you love him—that's obvious. Stay there with him. Make it work. You can practice from there just as well as you can here."

"It's not that simple. He deceived me. He knew Derek was alive."

"I'm sure he had his reasons," Donna said.

Cyanna didn't reply. There was a knock at her door. A nurse peeked in, rolling a machine behind her. "Donna, the nurse is here. I'll call you back after I'm discharged this afternoon."

"Sure. I'll talk to you later."

The nurse took Cyanna's blood pressure, temperature and other vital signs. When she left, Cyanna went into the bathroom to get the rest of her toiletries together. After a few minutes, she walked back into the room and stopped cold. There was a man standing there. He had his back to her, looking at the flowers. For a second she didn't recognize him, then her heart soared and she thought Mikhail had finally come. Then she realized it wasn't him. She whispered the man's name, "Derek."

He turned and smiled boyishly. "Hey, little sis," he said.

Tears rolled down Cyanna's cheeks. "Am I dreaming?" she said.

"I hope not."

She rushed over, charged into him and flung her arms around his neck tightly. She closed her eyes and silently thanked God for the gift of seeing her brother again. When she finally stepped back she touched his face tenderly. "How are you?"

"I'm back. But I should be asking you that question. You're the one in the hospital. How are you?"

She nodded, still teary-eyed. "Better, so much better."

"I'm glad to hear that."

Out of the blue she punched him in the arm. He smiled and chuckled with the same boyish charm that always melted her heart. "Oh my God, look at you. What did they do?"

"I'm fine. I just told you," he assured her.

"No, you're not fine. You're bruised and scarred and heaven knows what else they did to you. And dead, they said you were dead. I had a memorial service for you," she added, then punched him again. "You put me through hell."

"They were obviously mistaken. I'm sorry."

"Sorry isn't enough—they lied to me," she said.

"I know. It wasn't my decision. That was someone else."

"Yeah, obviously. So what happened to you? Are you okay? Where have you been all this time?"

"I was on assignment. It didn't go as expected. When the helicopter went down I—" She started crying again. "No, no, don't get upset. I hear you're supposed to be stress-free. I also hear I'm gonna be an uncle."

She hugged him again. "Where were you all this time?" He shook his head. "I hired a private investigator and one of his associates took a picture of you. He said you were captured and being held hostage. I was on my way to Bogotá."

"Bogotá?"

"Yes, that's where I thought you were."

"No, not Bogotá. This private investigator was obviously just conning you and taking your money."

"But he had a picture of you being held hostage. I saw you."

"It was probably doctored," he said. She sighed heavily. "When are you getting out of here?"

"Today, hopefully soon."

"And you are feeling better?"

She nodded. "Yes, much better."

"And your wrist?" he asked, looking down at the bandage.

"My wrist is getting better and stronger every day."

"Good. So are you going back to New York when you get out?"

"Yes."

"Are you sure—what about Mikhail?"

"How do you know about Mikhail? Wait a minute. How did you know about my blood pressure and the baby?" she added.

"Cyanna, I can't stay long. My ride is waiting for me outside. I'll be away for a few more days and then we'll talk."

"Where are you going?"

"I'll be back soon. I promise," he assured her.

She nodded, knowing he either had another job to do or he needed to meet with his superiors. They stood and she hugged him again. "Be safe."

"I will. Take care of yourself."

He stood and started across the room, then stopped

and turned to come back. He shook his head. "I can't," he said.

Cyanna stood. "What are you talking about? You can't what?"

"Sit down for a minute," he told her.

"Derek, what is it?"

"Sit down. We need to talk," he said. She sat back down. Her heart trembled. "I promised I wouldn't tell you, but I think you need to know. He loves you. I could see it in his eyes when he talked about you. He made me promise to watch out for you if anything—"

Cyanna's heart lurched. "Mikhail. What happened? Where is he?"

Derek nodded. "He came and got me out."

"What do you mean out? Out of where?"

Derek took a deep breath and sat next to his sister. "That doesn't matter. There was a confrontation," he began. Cyanna's eyes widened as she looked him over quickly. "No, no, I'm fine. I wasn't hit. Mikhail was—"

"What?" she rasped out slowly.

"Calm down," he said immediately, seeing the overwhelming concern in her face. "He didn't want me to tell you this because he knew you'd get upset. But I know you can handle it."

She took a deep breath, remembering her calming exercises, and nodded silently. "I'm fine. I'm fine. Just tell me what happened," Cyanna said slowly.

"Mikhail was hit in the exchange. He went down. I'm not sure of the extent of his injuries."

She shook her head, unbelieving. "What do you mean you're not sure? You were there, right?"

Derek nodded. "Yes, I was there. He was shot and then he fell. By the time we got to him he was…" He paused, seeing his sister's horrified reaction. "When I left, his brother was at his side."

"Dominik," she said. Derek nodded. "Where is he now, here in the hospital?" she asked anxiously.

"No, Dominik met up with us en route."

"Where did he take him?" she asked anxiously but still a lot calmer than even she expected.

"As far as I know, they were headed home." Derek's cell phone beeped. He looked at the caller ID. "I have to go. Are you going to be okay?" he asked.

She nodded. "Yes, go. Do what you have to do. I'll be fine."

He kissed her cheek, stood and walked out. Cyanna walked over to the bedside and picked up the hospital phone. The operator answered. "Yes, I need to be connected to Shauna Coles. It's an emergency." A few seconds later she was put through to Shauna's office.

"This is Shauna Coles."

"Shauna, it's Cyanna. I need to get out of here now."

Shauna paused a brief moment. "Cyanna…"

"It's not open for discussion. I need to get to Mikhail."

"Okay, I'll see what I can do."

Mikhail opened his eyes slowly and sat up. The movement stopped him in his tracks. A sharp stabbing pain shot into his side and shoulder simultaneously. He groaned and winced, taking a deep breath and releasing it slowly. He paused a few minutes to gather himself.

He looked around the room, recognizing he was still in his bedroom on Cutter Island.

His balcony doors were open, and a warm breeze was blowing into the room. It was daytime. He noticed his cell phone on the nightstand. He grabbed it and checked the time. It was eleven o'clock in the morning. He had been in bed for the past two days. It was time to get up, get off this rock and get back to his life. He sat up farther then stopped.

"Whoa. Whoa. Hey, slow down there. You need to take it easy for a while," Dominik said as he walked into the bedroom.

Mikhail looked across the room. "I'm fine," he gritted out tightly. "Just a little stiff getting up, that's all." The pain was just as intense as it was before, but this time he disregarded it. After a few deep breaths, he shifted off the bed, stood and took a few steps. Hearing laughter coming from outside, he glanced at the balcony doors, then continued to the bathroom. He stood at the counter.

"You shouldn't be getting up at all yet," Dominik called out. "You need at least another twenty-four hours' rest."

Mikhail signed heavily as he turned his face from side to side, looking at himself in the mirror. His hooded eyes were shadowed but revealed nothing of his days in South America.

He recalled what had happened the night they went in. They had done surveillance and it showed the area would have limited resistance. At one hundred yards they had their target. As soon as they had gotten eyes on the building, they moved in. They got Derek out. There was gunfire. Smoke. An explosion that rocked the small village. After that everything went sideways and it was pure chaos. One lucky shot clipped him in his side. It slammed him against a rock and he fell, dislocating his shoulder. But all in all stumbling out of a jungle in the dead of night was better than not getting out at all. They met the chopper and headed back across the border, then to the States and back home. And just like that it had been over.

Twenty minutes of insanity. They had what they had come for plus four other hostages, who turned out to be members of a UN peacekeeping operation. The State Department had been in stalled negotiations, but their operation cut to the chase and got them all out. Still, they knew this wasn't over. The State Department would be in contact with them, and official actions would be levied. They'd all be reprimanded, that was for sure, but rescuing the UN representatives would clear them instantly.

Mikhail rubbed at the new stubble on his face and decided it was time for a change. He shaved, leaving a goatee and mustache in place. He pulled the bandage from his side. He'd know his brother's stitches anywhere. They were tight, close-knit and neat, assuredly leaving the barest scar possible. He washed up and redressed his wounds. He put on some clothes and headed out into the great room. This was the strongest he'd felt in days. "What are you still doing here? I thought I told you to get back to Cyanna yesterday."

"Cyanna's fine. She's being discharged today. You,

on the other hand, aren't. You need to rest. I'm very proud of those stitches, and I have no intention of redoing them because you have a hard head and won't listen to sound medical advice."

"I hear you. I'm fine. You know this isn't my first rodeo."

"Yeah, yeah, whatever. How are you feeling?"

"Like I've been shot and then fell off a mountain."

Dominik chuckled. "Well, I guess that means that your memory's intact. That's exactly what happened."

He looked around the great room. Dominik was the only one there. "I heard laughter outside."

"David and Natalia are here with the boys," Dominik said. "They went down to the waterfall for a picnic. Nikita sent over lunch. You need to eat."

They went into the large kitchen. Mikhail sat down at the island counter, and Dominik pulled out two bottles of water. "Here you go—you need to hydrate."

"Thanks."

Dominik began pulling Nikita's lunch out of the warmer and the refrigerator. By the time he finished, there was a mountain of food covering the counters. "Jeez," Mikhail began. "It's only the four of us and the boys. How much did Nikita send over?"

"It looks like she sent everything in the kitchen. And actually, Shauna and the others will be here later this evening. We promised Mom and Dad we'd keep a close eye on you. That's the only way they'd go back to Marathon. So, what do you want to eat?"

"I'm not hungry," Mikhail said, taking another sip of water.

Dominik ignored him, knowing he had to eat something or pass out. "Like I said, we have everything—hot, cold, snacks, sandwiches, entrées, appetizers, desserts—basically the entire Nikita's Café menu, plus a few things I had no idea she made."

Mikhail took the last sip of his water, placed the empty bottle on the counter in front of him, then looked at his brother. "How is she?" he asked, knowing Dominik would know he was asking about Cyanna.

Dominik placed a second bottle of water and a sandwich he knew was one of his brother's favorites in front of him. "She's fine, and she'll be fine as long as she keeps her blood pressure under control."

He nodded assuredly, then took a bite of the large sandwich. "She will. I'll make sure of it."

"So, you want to tell me what you were thinking with this?"

Mikhail shook his head. "I have no idea," he confessed. "We met months ago when she had the memorial service for her brother."

"But he's not dead."

"Yeah, apparently when Derek's chopper went down she began making some folks very nervous with her questions, so some brilliant idiot stamped his file as deceased thinking that would keep her quiet," Mikhail said. Dominik shook his head. "I was sent to her to make sure she was okay. We had a connection that was scary crazy. That one weekend we talked, we loved, we laughed. It was like we'd known each other forever even though we'd just met. Like I said, scary crazy. I had to go. I walked away. When she came here, I couldn't walk away again. She wanted a baby, my baby, and I wanted her."

Dominik nodded. "Well, it will be great having another baby in the family."

Mikhail nodded and smiled unguardedly. "Yeah, I'm gonna be a dad and hopefully a husband." He paused. "I proposed to her."

Dominik smiled. "Yeah, I know. I saw the ring on her finger, but she didn't say anything about it."

"That's probably because she fell asleep before giving me her answer."

Dominik chuckled. "So what are you going to do?"

Mikhail looked at his brother. There was only one thing to do. "I'm going to shower, get dressed and head back to Key West. Then I'm gonna find Cyanna and move heaven and earth to have her in my life. I love her. She loves me. And with our child we're going to be a family," Mikhail said as he stood and headed back to the bedroom to put his plan in motion.

Dominik nodded and smiled his agreement. That's exactly what he wanted to hear. He pulled out his cell phone and called his wife. She answered on the first ring. "Shauna, I need you to get Cyanna here as soon as possible."

Chapter 16

The taxi barely stopped before Cyanna grabbed her bag, opened the door and got out. She paid and quickly climbed the steps and unlocked the front door. "Mikhail. Hello?" she called out as she stood in the foyer and looked around. The only answer was the echo of the empty house. She hurried up the staircase, calling out to him as she went. "Mikhail." She stormed into the bedroom and looked around frantically. He wasn't there, and it was obvious that he hadn't been there in a few days. She went back downstairs, continuing to the kitchen and back patio.

Derek had said Mikhail was home. Breathlessly, she hurried back to the staircase and headed up to the second floor. Midway she stopped and turned around. Her eyes lit up.

Just then the sound of a car pulling up in front got

her attention. She hurried to open the door, expecting to see Mikhail. Instead she saw Shauna getting out of her car and coming toward the house. "Hi, Shauna," she said, trying not to look as disappointed as she felt.

"Hey," Shauna said, hurrying up the steps. "I hoped I'd find you here. I tried to catch you before you left the hospital."

"Mikhail isn't here. I have no idea where he is," Cyanna said.

"I do. I'm on my way there now. He's at Cutter Island."

Cyanna brightened instantly. "Shauna, I need to see him. Can you help me?"

"Yes, I know. Come on—I'll drive to the marina. Tatiana is waiting to take us over as soon as we get there."

She ran back to the house to grab her things. Her heart pounded with joy, and as much as she tried to calm herself, she was just too excited and apprehensive. "How is he, Shauna?" she asked, not sure she was ready to hear the answer.

"I don't know. I haven't seen him. I know he was hit and he lost blood. Dominik's still with him."

Cyanna heard the words but this time she refused to let them seep in. They drove the rest of the way in silence. Shauna parked in the private lot behind the bungalows. They got out. Cyanna looked around, not sure which way to go. "This way," Shauna said. Cyanna nodded and followed quickly. They met Tatiana and Nikita waiting on the docks. They all got into the boat, and Tatiana headed to Cutter Island.

The twenty-minute boat ride seemed to take an eternity. Shauna and Nikita stayed with her down on the lower deck, while Tatiana drove the boat as if she'd been born to it. The boat soared over and cut through the crashing waves. She finally saw a small land mass on the far horizon. She knew it was Cutter Island and it made her even more anxious. She had prayed all her life to find someone to feel safe with, and God had answered her prayers in Mikhail. With him she had everything she ever wanted. He was kind, generous, loving and most definitely the only man for her, and she knew she was the only woman for him. She just hoped it wasn't too late.

When they got close, Tatiana slowed their approach, steering the boat alongside the dock. Two other boats were already there. Nikita jumped down and secured the boat as Shauna and Cyanna hurried up the path to the house. Well up the path, Cyanna turned to thank the sisters for bringing her.

Seeing them coming from the dock, Dominik opened the front door. "Welcome. Come in," he said to Cyanna. Shauna followed, smiling at her husband.

"Thank you." Cyanna walked inside and looked around for Mikhail. He wasn't there. But she knew wherever Dominik was Mikhail was close by.

"How are you feeling?" Dominik asked.

"I don't know yet," she said.

He knew she was referring to not seeing Mikhail. "If you like, I can take that bandage off your hand and wrist now."

She nodded impatiently. "Later. Where is—"

"He's in his bedroom, third room on the left."

Cyanna crossed the great room quickly, following Dominik's directions. She stopped at Mikhail's bedroom door. It was already open. She walked inside and looked around. The bed had been slept in and she recognized Mikhail's cell phone on the nightstand. Her heart pounded excitedly. Thin sheers at the balcony doors blew with the breeze. She remembered the billowing sheers and finding him outside one night when it had rained. She walked over and saw the man she loved standing outside. Her heart leaped. She stepped on the balcony just as he turned around. His eyes lit up. "Cyanna," he whispered.

She smiled as tears rolled down her cheeks. She looked at him head to barefoot toe. He was okay. He wore jeans and no shirt. His one shoulder was badly bruising, red and turning blue. There was a wide white bandage on the side of his body. He was alive and that's all that mattered. She took two quick, halted breaths, then ran into his arms.

Mikhail caught her as pain shot through his shoulder and side, but he didn't care. He didn't even feel it. All he felt was his heart's desire in knowing Cyanna was there with him. He held her tight, hoping this was the beginning of their life together. "Cyanna, I love you."

"I love you," she whispered.

"Don't ever leave me again."

She leaned back and smiled. "Where would I go? My life is here with you and our child." They kissed, and the world seemed to brighten as warm sunshine beamed down on them. "I had a dream."

"What kind of dream?" he asked.

"A good one," she said. "In it you asked me to marry you."

"And in this dream, what was your answer?"

"Yes."

He nodded. "Good. That's good to know."

"Yeah, I think so, too."

"So." He released her and knelt down on one knee. "Cyanna Dupres, will you do me the honor of becoming my wife?"

She smiled and nodded joyfully. "Yes, yes, yes." She pulled him up, and they kissed passionately. Afterward she looked up at him and smiled. "And since I already have the ring," she said, holding her hand up and the bandage back to show him the ring he placed on her finger days earlier.

He smiled. "You knew. You remembered."

She nodded. "Yes. Not that night, but the next day. That's why I was looking for you to come see me. But you didn't. Your phone was turned off."

"I was kind of busy."

"Yeah, saving my brother and getting shot."

"All in a day's work," he said.

She shook her head. "Not anymore," she said. "You're gonna be a husband and a dad."

He nodded in complete agreement. "You're absolutely right, not anymore," he said.

"Hey, can we come back in now?"

Mikhail and Cyanna looked down over the balcony and saw the Coles family with husbands, wives and children looking up at them. They smiled and waved.

"Yeah, come on up. We're celebrating. We're getting married."

The cheer of joy and excitement echoed across the small island. The family came up to congratulate them. Dominik removed Cyanna's bandage and the ring Mikhail had placed on her finger sparkled anew.

The family celebration was beyond awesome. By sunset more members of the Coles family had arrived on the island and the evening turned into a huge holiday, celebrating family and love.

Later that night Mikhail and Cyanna said their goodbyes to the family and watched as they got into their boats and headed back to Key West. Mikhail and Cyanna went back to the house and stood out on his balcony, where they had pledged their love eternally. She wrapped her arm around his body, and he held her close. "It's so beautiful here on Cutter, and I'm so happy. I never want this moment to end."

"But it will, and we'll have thousands and thousands more incredible moments to share with our family." She stood in front of him as he caressed her stomach.

"So, tell me, what exactly was the last term?" she asked.

"This, you and me, together forever. How does that sound?"

"Hmm," she began. "Well, I think I can agree to that."

"Good. I love you, soon-to-be Mrs. Mikhail Coles."

She smiled, deliriously happy. "I love you, too, Mr. Coles."

They looked off over the trees, seeing the last family boat sail toward the horizon, leaving them on Cutter Island alone. "This is only the beginning of our Coles family story. With our children and our children's children, there will be so much more to come."

"I like the sound of that," Cyanna said as she turned into his embrace and kissed him. She knew that in Mikhail she had everything she'd always wanted—the true love of her life forever and ever.

* * * * *

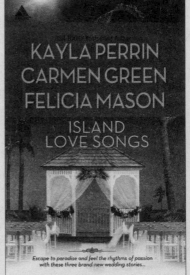

The perfect stories to indulge in...

Hollington Homecoming
VOLUME ONE

SANDRA KITT
ESSENCE BESTSELLING AUTHOR
JACQUELIN THOMAS

Experience the drama and
passion as eight friends
reunite in Atlanta for their
ten-year college reunion!
This collection features the
first two full-length novels in
the Hollington Homecoming
series, *RSVP with Love*
by Sandra Kitt and
Teach Me Tonight by
Jacquelin Thomas.

"This heartwarming story has characters that grow and
mature beautifully."
—*RT Book Reviews* on *RSVP WITH LOVE*

Available August 2013 wherever books are sold!

And coming in September, HOLLINGTON HOMECOMING VOLUME TWO,
featuring Pamela Yaye and Adrianne Byrd

HARLEQUIN®
™ www.Harlequin.com

KPHH10813

REQUEST YOUR FREE BOOKS!

2 FREE NOVELS PLUS 2 **FREE GIFTS!**

KIMANI™
ROMANCE

Love's ultimate destination!

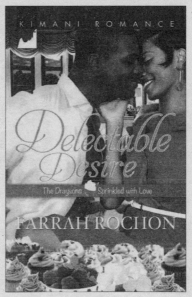 

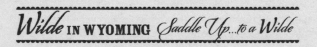

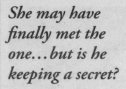